The licence to kill for the Secret Service, the double-O prefix, was a great honour. It had been earned hardly. It brought James Bond the only assignments he enjoyed – the dangerous ones

CASINO ROYALE

LIVE AND LET DIE

MOONRAKER

DIAMONDS ARE FOREVER

FROM RUSSIA, WITH LOVE

DR NO

GOLDFINGER

FOR YOUR EYES ONLY

THUNDERBALL

ON HER MAJESTY'S SECRET SERVICE

YOU ONLY LIVE TWICE

These eleven James Bond novels have so far appeared as Pan Books. The titles shown in bold type have been filmed by Eon Films, starring Sean Connery as 007. The fifth film, YOU ONLY LIVE TWICE, will be released this year.

YOU ONLY LIVE TWICE

IAN FLEMING

UNABRIDGED

PAN BOOKS LTD : LONDON

First published 1964 by Jonathan Cape Ltd.
This edition published 1965 by Pan Books Ltd.,
8 Headfort Place, London, S.W.1

2nd Printing 1966
3rd Printing 1966

© Glidrose Productions Ltd., 1964

Printed in Great Britain by Richard Clay (The Chaucer Press), Ltd.,
Bungay, Suffolk

CONTENTS

To
Richard Hughes
and
Torao Saito

But
for
whom
etc. . . .

You only live twice:
Once when you are born
And once when you look death in the face.

After BASHŌ
Japanese poet,
1643–94

Part One

'It is
better
to
travel
hopefully . . .

1

SCISSORS CUT PAPER

THE geisha called 'Trembling Leaf', on her knees beside James Bond, leant forward from the waist and kissed him chastely on the right cheek.

'That's a cheat,' said Bond severely. 'You agreed that if I won it would be a real kiss on the mouth. At the very least,' he added.

'Grey Pearl', the Madame, who had black lacquered teeth, a bizarre affectation, and was so thickly made up that she looked like a character out of a No play, translated. There was much giggling and cries of encouragement. Trembling Leaf covered her face with her pretty hands as if she were being required to perform some ultimate obscenity. But then the fingers divided and the pert brown eyes examined Bond's mouth, as if taking aim, and her body lanced forward. This time the kiss was full on the lips and it lingered fractionally. In invitation? In promise? Bond remembered that he had been promised a 'pillow geisha'. Technically, this would be a geisha of low caste. She would not be proficient in the traditional arts of her calling – she would not be able to tell humorous stories, sing, paint or compose verses about her patron. But, unlike her cultured sisters, she might agree to perform more robust services – discreetly, of course, in conditions of the utmost privacy and at a high price. But, to the boorish, brutalized tastes of a *gaijin*, a foreigner, this made more sense than having a *tanka* of thirty-one syllables, which in any case he couldn't understand, equate, in exquisite ideograms, his charms with budding chrysanthemums on the slopes of Mount Fuji.

The applause which greeted this unbridled exhibition of lasciviousness died quickly and respectfully. The powerful, chunky man in the black *yukata*, sitting directly across the low red lacquer table from Bond, had taken the Dunhill filter holder from between his golden teeth and had laid it beside his ashtray. 'Bondo-san,' said Tiger Tanaka, Head of the Japanese Secret Service, 'I will now challenge you to this ridiculous game, and I promise you in advance that you will not win.' The big, creased brown face that Bond had come to know so well in the past month split expansively. The wide smile closed the almond eyes to slits – slits that glittered. Bond knew that smile. It wasn't a smile. It was a mask with a golden hole in it.

Bond laughed. 'All right, Tiger. But first, more *sake*! And not in these ridiculous thimbles. I've drunk five flasks of the stuff and its effect is about the same as one double Martini. I shall need another double Martini if I am to go on demonstrating the superiority of Western instinct over the wiles of the Orient. Is there such a thing as a lowly glass tumbler discarded in some corner behind the cabinets of Ming?'

'Bondo-san. Ming is Chinese. Your knowledge of porcelain is as meagre as your drinking habits are gross. Moreover, it is unwise to underestimate *sake*. We have a saying, "It is the man who drinks the first flask of *sake*; then the second flask drinks the first; then it is the *sake* that drinks the man."' Tiger Tanaka turned to Grey Pearl and there followed a laughing conversation which Bond interpreted as jokes at the expense of this uncouth Westerner and his monstrous appetites. At a word from the Madame, Trembling Leaf bowed low and scurried out of the room. Tiger turned to Bond. 'You have gained much face, Bondo-san. It is only the *sumo* wrestlers who drink *sake* in these quantities without showing it. She says you are undoubtedly an eight-flask man.' Tiger's face became sly. 'But she also suggests that you will not make much of a companion for Trembling Leaf at the end of the evening.'

'Tell her that I am more interested in her own more mature charms. She will certainly possess talents in the art of love making which will overcome any temporary lassitude on my part.'

This leaden gallantry got what it deserved. There came a spirited crackle of Japanese from Grey Pearl. Tiger translated.

'Bondo-san, this is a woman of some wit. She has made a joke. She says she is already respectably married to one *bonsan* and there is no room on her *futon* for another. *Bonsan* means a priest, a greybeard. *Futon*, as you know, is a bed. She has made a joke on your name.'

The geisha party had been going on for two hours, and Bond's jaws were aching with the unending smiles and polite repartee. Far from being entertained by the geisha, or bewitched by the inscrutable discords issuing from the catskin-covered box of the three-stringed *samisen,* Bond had found himself having to try desperately to make the party go. He also knew that Tiger Tanaka had been observing his effort with a sadistic pleasure. Dikko Henderson had warned him that geisha parties were more or less the equivalent, for a foreigner, of trying to entertain a lot of unknown children in a nursery with a strict governess, the Madame, looking on. But Dikko had also warned him that he was being done a great honour by Tiger Tanaka, that the party would cost Tiger a small fortune, whether from secret funds or from his own pocket, and that Bond had better put a good face on the whole thing since this looked like being a breakthrough in Bond's mission. But it could equally well be disaster.

So now Bond smiled and clapped his hands in admiration. He said to Tiger, 'Tell the old bitch she's a clever old bitch,' accepted the brimming tumbler of hot *sake* from the apparently adoring hands of Trembling Leaf, and downed it in two tremendous gulps. He repeated the performance so that more *sake* had to be fetched from the kitchen, then he placed his fist decisively on the red lacquer table and said with mock belligerence, 'All right, Tiger! Go to it!'

It was the old game of Scissors cut Paper, Paper wraps Stone, Stone blunts Scissors, that is played by children all over the world. The fist is the Stone, two outstretched fingers are the Scissors, and a flat hand is the Paper. The closed fist is hammered twice in the air simultaneously by the two opponents and, at the third downward stroke, the chosen emblem is revealed. The game consists of guessing which emblem the opponent will choose, and of you yourself choosing one that will defeat him. Best of three goes or more. It is a game of bluff.

Tiger Tanaka rested his fist on the table opposite Bond. The two men looked carefully into each other's eyes. There was dead silence in the box-like little lath-and-paper room, and the soft gurgling of the tiny brook in the ornamental square of garden outside the opened partition could be heard clearly for the first time that evening. Perhaps it was this silence, after all the talk and giggling, or perhaps it was the deep seriousness and purpose that was suddenly evident in Tiger Tanaka's formidable, cruel, *samurai* face, but Bond's skin momentarily crawled. For some reason this had become more than a children's game. Tiger had promised he would beat Bond. To fail would be to lose much face. How much? Enough to breach a friendship that had become oddly real between the two of them over the past weeks? This was one of the most powerful men in Japan. To be defeated by a miserable *gaijin* in front of the two women might be a matter of great moment to this man. The defeat might leak out through the women. In the West, such a trifle would be farcically insignificant, like a cabinet minister losing a game of backgammon at Blades. But in the East? In a very short while, Dikko Henderson had taught Bond total respect for Oriental conventions, however old-fashioned or seemingly trivial, but Bond was still at sea in their gradations. This was a case in point. Should Bond try and win at this baby game of bluff and double-bluff, or should he try to lose? But to try and lose involved the same cleverness at correctly guessing the other man's symbols in advance. It was just as difficult to lose on purpose as to win. And anyway did it really matter? Unfortunately, on the curious assignment in which James Bond was involved, he had a nasty feeling that even this idiotic little gambit had significance towards success or failure.

As if with second sight, Tiger Tanaka spelled the problem out. He gave a harsh, taut laugh that was more of a shout than an expression of humour or pleasure. 'Bondo-san, with us, and certainly at a party at which I am the host and you are the honoured guest, it would be good manners for me to let you win this game that we are to play together. It would be more. It would be required behaviour. So I must ask your forgiveness in advance for defeating you.'

Bond smiled cheerfully. 'My dear Tiger, there is no point in playing a game unless you try to win. It would be a very great insult to me if you endeavoured to play to lose. But if I may say so, your remarks are highly provocative. They are like the taunts of the *sumo* wrestlers before the bout. If I was not myself so certain of winning, I would point out that you spoke in English. Please tell our dainty and distinguished audience that I propose to rub your honourable nose in the dirt at this despicable game and thus display not only the superiority of Great Britain, and particularly Scotland, over Japan, but also the superiority of our Queen over your Emperor.' Bond, encouraged perhaps by the crafty ambush of the *sake*, had committed himself. This kind of joking about their different cultures had become a habit between himself and Tiger, who, with a first in PPE at Trinity before the war, prided himself in the *demokorasu* of his outlook and the liberality and breadth of his understanding of the West. But Bond, having spoken, caught the sudden glitter in the dark eyes, and he thought of Dikko Henderson's cautionary, 'Now listen, you stupid limey bastard. You're doing all right. But don't press your luck. T.T.'s a civilized kind of a chap – as Japs go, that is. But don't overdo it. Take a look at that mug. There's Manchu there, and Tartar. And don't forget the soanso was a Black Belt at judo before he ever went up to your bloody Oxford. And don't forget he was spying for Japan when he called himself assistant naval attaché in their London Embassy before the war and you stupid bastards thought he was okay because he'd got a degree at Oxford. And don't forget his war record. Don't forget he ended up as personal aide to Admiral Ohnishi and was training as a *kami-kaze* when the Americans made loud noises over Nagasaki and Hiroshima and the Rising Sun suddenly took a backward somersault in to the sea. And, if you forget all that, just ask yourself why it's T.T. rather than any other of the ninety million Japanese who happens to hold down the job as head of the *Kōan-Chōsa-Kyōku*. Okay, James? Got the photo?'

Since Bond had arrived in Japan he had assiduously practised sitting in the lotus position. Dikko Henderson had advised it. 'If you make the grade with these people,' he had said, 'or even if you don't, you'll be spending a lot of time sitting on your ass on the ground. There's only one way to do it without cracking your joints; that's in the Indian position, squatting with your legs crossed and the sides of your feet hurting like hell on the floor. It takes a bit of practice, but it won't kill you and you'll end up gaining plenty of face.' Bond had more or less mastered the art, but now, after two hours, his kneejoints were on fire and he felt that if he didn't alter his posture he would end up bandy-legged for life. He said to Tiger, 'Playing against a master such as yourself, I must first adopt a relaxed position so that my brain may be totally concentrated.' He got painfully to his feet, stretched and sat down again – this time with one leg extended under the low table and his left elbow resting on the bent knee of the other. It was a blessed relief. He lifted his tumbler and, obediently, Trembling Leaf filled it from a fresh flagon. Bond downed the *sake*, handed the tumbler to the girl and suddenly crashed his right fist down on the lacquer table so that the little boxes of sweetmeats rattled and the porcelain tinkled. He looked belligerently across at Tiger Tanaka. 'Right!'

Tiger bowed. Bond bowed back. The girl leant forward expectantly.

Tiger's eyes bored into Bond's, trying to read his plan. Bond had decided to have no plan, display no pattern. He would play completely at random, showing the symbol that his fist decided to make at the psychological moment after the two hammer blows.

Tiger said, 'Three games of three?'

'Right.'

The two fists rose slowly from the table top, quickly hammered twice in unison and shot forward. Tiger had kept his fist balled in the Stone. Bond's palm was open in the Paper that wrapped the Stone. One up to Bond. Again the ritual and the moment of truth. Tiger had kept to the Stone. Bond's first and second fingers were open in the Scissors, blunted by Tiger's Stone. One all.

Tiger paused and placed his fist against his forehead. He closed his eyes in thought. He said, 'Yes. I've got you, Bondo-san. You can't escape.'

'Good show,' said Bond, trying to clear his mind of the suspicion that Tiger would keep to the Stone, or alternatively, that Tiger would expect him to play it that way, expect Bond to play the Paper and himself riposte with the Scissors to cut the paper. And so on and so forth. The three emblems whirled round in Bond's mind like the symbols on a fruit machine.

The two fists were raised – one, two, forward!

Tiger had kept to his Stone. Bond had wrapped it up with the Paper. First game to Bond.

The second game lasted longer. They both kept on showing the same symbol, which meant a replay. It was as if the two players were getting the measure of each other's psychology. But that could not be so, since Bond had no psychological intent. He continued to play at random. It was just luck. Tiger won the game. One all.

Last game! The two contestants looked at each other. Bond's smile was bland, rather mocking. A glint of red shone in the depths of Tiger's dark eyes. Bond saw it and said to himself, 'I would be wise to lose. Or would I?' He won the game in two straight goes, blunting Tiger's Scissors with his Stone, wrapping Tiger's Stone with his Paper.

Tiger bowed low. Bond bowed even lower. He sought for a throwaway remark. He said, 'I must get this game adopted in time for your Olympics. I would certainly be chosen to play for my country.'

Tiger Tanaka laughed with controlled politeness. 'You play with much insight. What was the secret of your method?'

Bond had had no method. He quickly invented the one that would be most polite to Tiger. 'You are a man of rock and steel, Tiger. I guessed that the paper symbol would be the one you would use the least. I played accordingly.'

This bit of mumbo-jumbo got by. Tiger bowed. Bond bowed and drank more *sake*, toasting Tiger. Released from the tension, the geisha applauded and the Madame instructed Trembling Leaf to give Bond another kiss. She did so. How soft the skins of Japanese women were! And their touch was almost weightless! James Bond was plotting the rest of his night when Tiger said, 'Bondo-san, I have matters to discuss with you. Will you do me the honour of coming to my house for a nightcap?'

Bond immediately put away his lascivious thoughts. According to Dikko, to be invited to a Japanese private house was a most unusual sign of favour. So, for some reason, he had done right to win this childish game. This might mean great things. Bond bowed. 'Nothing would give me more pleasure, Tiger.'

An hour later they were sitting in blessed chairs with a drink-tray between them. The lights of Yokohama glowed a deep orange along the horizon, and a slight smell of the harbour and the sea came in through the wide-open partition leading on to the garden. Tiger's house was designed, enchantingly, as is even the meanest Japanese salary-man's house, to establish the thinnest possible dividing line between the inhabitant and nature. The three other partitions in the square room were also fully slid back, revealing a bedroom, a small study and a passage.

Tiger had opened the partitions when they entered the room. He had commented, 'In the West, when you have secrets to discuss, you shut all the doors and windows. In Japan, we throw everything open to make sure that no one can listen at the thin walls. And what I have now to discuss with you is a matter of the very highest secrecy. The *sake* is warm enough? You have the cigarettes you prefer? Then listen to what I have to say to you and swear on your honour to divulge it to no one.' Tiger Tanaka gave his great golden shout of mirthless laughter. 'If you were to break your promise, I would have no alternative but to remove you from the earth.'

2

CURTAINS FOR BOND?

EXACTLY one month before, it had been the eve of the annual closing of Blades. On the next day, 1 September, those members who were still unfashionably in London would have to pig it for a month at Whites or Boodle's. Whites they considered noisy and 'smart', Boodle's too full of superannuated country squires who would be talking of nothing but the opening of the partridge season. For Blades, it was one month in the wilderness. But there it was. The staff, one supposed, had to have their holiday. More important, there was some painting to be done and there was dry-rot in the roof.

M., sitting in the bow window looking out over St James's Street, couldn't care less. He had two weeks' trout fishing on the Test to look forward to and, for the other two weeks, he would have sandwiches and coffee at his desk. He rarely used Blades, and then only to entertain important guests. He was not a 'clubable' man and if he had had the choice he would have stuck to The Senior, that greatest of all Services' clubs in the world. But too many people knew him there, and there was too much 'shop' talked. And there were too many former shipmates who *would* come up and ask him what he had been doing with himself since he retired. And the lie, 'Got a job with some people called Universal Export,' bored him, and though verifiable, had its risks.

Porterfield hovered with the cigars. He bent and offered the wide case to M.'s guest. Sir James Molony raised a quizzical eyebrow. 'I see the Havanas are still coming in.' His hand hesitated. He picked out a Romeo y Julieta, pinched it gently and ran it under his nose. He turned to M. 'What's Universal Export sending Castro in return? Blue Streak?'

M. was not amused. Porterfield observed that he wasn't. As Chief Petty Officer, he had served under M. in one of his last commands. He said quickly, but not too quickly, 'As a matter of fact, Sir James, the best of the Jamaicans are quite up to the Havanas these days. They've got the outer leaf just right at last.' He closed the glass lid of the case and moved away.

Sir James Molony picked up the piercer the head waiter had left on the table and punctured the tip of his cigar with precision. He lit a Swan Vesta and waved its flame to and fro across the tip and sucked gently until he had got the cigar going to his satisfaction. Then he took a sip, first at his brandy and then at his coffee, and sat back. He observed the corrugated brow of his host with affection and irony. He said, 'All right, my friend. Now tell me. What's the problem?'

M.'s mind was elsewhere. He seemed to be having difficulty getting his pipe going. He said vaguely, between puffs, 'What problem?'

Sir James Molony was the greatest neurologist in England. The year before, he had been awarded a Nobel Prize for his now famous *Some Psychosomatic Side-effects of Organic Inferiority*. He was also nerve specialist by appointment to the Secret Service and, though he was rarely called in, and then only *in extremis*, the problems he was required to solve intrigued him greatly because they were both human and vital to the State. And, since the war, the second qualification was a rare one.

M. turned sideways to his guest and watched the traffic up St James's.

Sir James Molony said, 'My friend, like everybody else, you have certain patterns of behaviour. One of them consists of occasionally asking me to lunch at Blades, stuffing me like a Strasbourg goose, and then letting me in on some ghastly secret and asking me to help you with it. The last time, as I recall, you wanted to find out if I could extract certain information from a foreign diplomat by getting him under deep hypnosis without his knowledge. You said it was a last resort. I said I couldn't help you. Two weeks later, I read in the paper that this same diplomat had come to a fatal end by experimenting with the force of gravity from a tenth floor window. The coroner gave an open verdict of the "Fell Or Was Pushed" variety. What song am I to sing for my supper this time?'

Sir James Molony relented. He said with sympathy, 'Come on, M.! Get it off your chest!'

M. looked him coldly in the eye. 'It's 007. I'm getting more and more worried about him.'

'You've read my two reports on his condition. Anything new?'

'No. Just the same. He's going slowly to pieces. Late at the office. Skimps his work. Makes mistakes. He's drinking too much and losing a lot of money at one of these new gambling clubs. It all adds up to the fact that one of my best men is on the edge of becoming a security risk. Absolutely incredible considering his record.'

Sir James Molony shook his head with conviction. 'It's not in the least incredible. You either don't read my reports or you don't pay enough attention to them. I have said all along that the man is suffering from shock.' Sir James Molony leant forward and pointed his cigar at M.'s chest. 'You're a hard man, M. In your job you have to be. But there are some problems, the human ones for instance, that you can't always solve with a rope's end. This is a case in point. Here's this agent of yours, just as tough and brave as I expect you were at his age. He's a bachelor and a confirmed womanizer. Then he suddenly falls in love, partly, I suspect, because this woman was a bird with a wing down and needed his help. It's surprising what soft centres these so-called tough men always have. So he marries her and within a few hours she's shot dead by this super-gangster chap. What was his name?'

'Blofeld,' said M. 'Ernst Stavro Blofeld.'

'All right. And your man got away with nothing worse than a crack on the head. But then he started going to pieces and your MO thought he might have suffered some brain injury and sent him along to me. Nothing wrong with him at all. Nothing physical that is – just shock. He admitted to me that all his zest had gone. That he wasn't interested in his job any more, or even in his life. I hear this sort of talk from patients every day. It's a form of psycho-neurosis, and it can grow slowly or suddenly. In your man's case, it was brought on out of the blue by an intolerable life-situation – or one that he found intolerable because he had never encountered it before – the loss of a loved one, aggravated in his case by the fact that he blamed himself for her death. Now, my friend, neither you nor I have had to carry such a burden, so we don't know how we would react under it. But I can tell you that it's a hell of a burden to lug around. And your man's caving in under it. I thought, and I said so in my report, that his job, its dangers and emergencies and so forth, would shake him out of it. I've found that one must try and teach people that there's no top limit to disaster – that, so long as breath remains in your body, you've got to accept the miseries of life. They will often seem infinite, insupportable. They are part of the human condition. Have you tried him on any tough assignments in the last few months?'

'Two,' said M. drearily. 'He bungled them both. On one he nearly got himself killed, and on the other he made a mistake that was dangerous for others. That's another thing that worries me. He didn't make mistakes before. Now suddenly he's become accident-prone.'

'Another symptom of his neurosis. So what are you going to do about it?'

'Fire him,' said M. brutally. 'Just as if he'd been shot to pieces or got some incurable disease. I've got no room in his Section for a lame-brain, whatever his past record or whatever excuses you psychologists can find for him. Pension, of course. Honourable discharge and all that. Try and find him a job. One of these new security organizations for the banks might take him.' M. looked defensively into the clear blue, comprehending eyes of the famous neurologist. He said, seeking support for his decision, 'You do see my point, Sir James? I'm tightly staffed at Headquarters, and in the field, for that matter. There's just no place where I can tuck away 007 so that he won't cause harm.'

'You'll be losing one of your best men.'

'Used to be. Isn't any longer.'

Sir James Molony sat back. He looked out of the window and puffed thoughtfully at his cigar. He liked this man Bond. He had had him as his patient perhaps a dozen times before.

He had seen how the spirit, the reserves in the man, could pull him out of badly damaged conditions that would have broken the normal human being. He knew how a desperate situation would bring out those reserves again, how the will to live would spring up again in a real emergency. He remembered how countless neurotic patients had disappeared for ever from his consulting-rooms when the last war had broken out. The big worry had driven out the smaller ones, the greater fear the lesser. He made up his mind. He turned back to M. 'Give him one more chance, M. If it'll help, I'll take the responsibility.'

'What sort of chance are you thinking of?'

'Well now, I don't know much about your line of business, M. And I don't want to. Got enough secrets in my own job to look after. But haven't you got something really sticky, some apparently hopeless assignment you can give this man? I don't mean necessarily dangerous, like assassination or stealing Russian ciphers or whatever. But something that's desperately important but apparently impossible. By all means give him a kick in the pants at the same time if you want to, but what he needs most of all is a supreme call on his talents, something that'll really make him sweat so that he's simply forced to forget his personal troubles. He's a patriotic sort of a chap. Give him something that really matters to his country. It would be easy enough if a war broke out. Nothing like death or glory to take a man out of himself. But can't you dream up something that simply stinks of urgency? If you can, give him the job. It might get him right back on the rails. Anyway, give him the chance. Yes?'

The urgent thrill of the red telephone, that had been silent for so many weeks, shot Mary Goodnight out of her seat at the typewriter as if it had been fitted with a cartridge ejector. She dashed through into the next room, waited a second to get her breath back and picked up the receiver as if it had been a rattlesnake.

'Yes, sir.'

'No, sir. It's his secretary speaking.' She looked down at her watch, knowing the worst.

'It's most unusual, sir. I don't expect he'll be more than a few minutes. Shall I ask him to call you, sir?'

'Yes, sir.' She put the receiver back on its cradle. She noticed that her hand was trembling. Damn the man! Where the hell was he? She said aloud, 'Oh, James, please hurry.' She walked disconsolately back and sat down again at her empty typewriter. She gazed at the grey keys with unseeing eyes and broadcast with all her telepathic strength, 'James! James! M. wants you! M. wants you! M. wants you!' Her heart dropped a beat. The Syncraphone. Perhaps just this once he hadn't forgotten it. She hurried back into his room and tore open the right hand drawer. No! There it was, the little plastic receiver on which he could have been bleeped by the switchboard. The gadget that it was mandatory for all senior Headquarters staff to carry when they left the building. But for weeks he had been forgetting to carry it, or worse, not caring if he did or didn't. She took it out and slammed it down in the centre of his blotter. 'Oh, damn you! Damn you! Damn you!' she said out loud, and walked back into her room with dragging feet.

The state of your health, the state of the weather, the wonders of nature – these are things that rarely occupy the average man's mind until he reaches the middle thirties. It is only on the threshold of middle-age that you don't take them all for granted, just part of an unremarkable background to more urgent, more interesting things.

Until this year, James Bond had been more or less oblivious to all of them. Apart from occasional hangovers, and the mending of physical damage that was merely, for him, the extension of a child falling down and cutting its knee, he had taken good health for granted. The weather? Just a question of whether or not he had to carry a raincoat or put the hood up on his Bentley Convertible. As for birds, bees and flowers, the wonders of nature, it only mattered whether or not they bit or stung, whether they smelled good or bad. But today, on the last day of August, just eight months, as he had reminded himself that morning, since Tracy had died, he sat in Queen

Mary's Rose Garden in Regent's Park, and his mind was totally occupied with just these things.

First his health. He felt like hell and knew that he also looked it. For months, without telling anyone, he had tramped Harley Street, Wigmore Street and Wimpole Street looking for any kind of doctor who would make him feel better. He had appealed to specialists, GPs, quacks – even to a hypnotist. He had told them, 'I feel like hell. I sleep badly. I eat practically nothing. I drink too much and my work has gone to blazes. I'm shot to pieces. Make me better.' And each man had taken his blood pressure, a specimen of his urine, listened to his heart and chest, asked him questions he had answered truthfully, and had told him there was nothing basically wrong with him. Then he had paid his five guineas and gone off to John Bell and Croyden to have the new lot of prescriptions – for tranquillizers, sleeping pills, energizers – made up. And now he had just come from breaking off relations with the last resort – the hypnotist, whose basic message had been that he must go out and regain his manhood by having a woman. As if he hadn't tried that! The ones who had told him to take it easy up the stairs. The ones who had asked him to take them to Paris. The ones who had inquired indifferently, 'Feeling better now, dearie?' The hypnotist hadn't been a bad chap. Rather a bore about how he could take away warts and how he was persecuted by the BMA, but Bond had finally had enough of sitting in a chair and listening to the quietly droning voice while, as instructed, he relaxed and gazed at a naked electric light bulb. And now he had thrown up the fifty-guinea course after only half the treatment and had come to sit in this secluded garden before going back to his office ten minutes away across the park.

He looked at his watch. Just after three o'clock, and he was due back at two-thirty. What the hell! God, it was hot. He wiped a hand across his forehead and then down the side of his trousers. He used not to sweat like this. The weather must be changing. Atomic bomb, whatever the scientists might say to the contrary. It would be good to be down somewhere in the South of France. Somewhere to bathe whenever he wanted. But he had had his leave for the year. That ghastly month they had given him after Tracy. Then he had gone to Jamaica. And what hell that had been. No! Bathing wasn't the answer. It was all right here, really. Lovely roses to look at. They smelled good and it was pleasant looking at them and listening to the faraway traffic. Nice hum of bees. The way they went around the flowers, doing their work for their queen. Must read that book about them by the Belgian chap, Metternich or something. Same man who wrote about the ants. Extraordinary purpose in life. They didn't have troubles. Just lived and died. Did what they were supposed to do and then dropped dead. Why didn't one see a lot of bees' corpses around? Ants' corpses? Thousands, millions of them must die every day. Perhaps the others ate them. Oh, well! Better go back to the office and get hell from Mary. She was a darling. She was right to nag at him as she did. She was his conscience. But she didn't realize the troubles he had. What troubles? Oh well. Don't let's go into that! James Bond got to his feet and went over and read the lead labels of the roses he had been gazing at. They told him that the bright vermilion ones were 'Super Star' and the white ones 'Iceberg'.

Then, with a jumble of his health, the heat, and the corpses of bees revolving lazily round his mind, James Bond strolled off in the direction of the tall grey building whose upper storeys showed themselves above the trees.

It was three thirty. Only two more hours to go before his next drink!

The lift man, resting the stump of his right arm on the operating handle, said, 'Your secretary's in a bit of a flap, sir. Been asking everywhere for you.'

'Thank you, Sergeant.'

He got the same message when he stepped out at the fifth floor and showed his pass to the security guard at the desk. He walked unhurriedly along the quiet corridor to the group of end rooms whose outer door bore the Double-O sign. He went through and along to the door marked 007. He closed it behind him. Mary Goodnight looked up at him and said calmly, 'M. wants you. He rang down half an hour ago.'

'Who's M.?'

Mary Goodnight jumped to her feet, her eyes flashing. 'Oh for God's sake, James, snap out of it! Here, your tie's crooked.' She came up to him and he docilely allowed her to pull it straight. 'And your hair's all over the place. Here, use my comb.' Bond took the comb and ran it absent-mindedly through his hair. He said, 'You're a good girl, Goodnight.' He fingered his chin. 'Suppose you haven't got your razor handy? Must look my best on the scaffold.'

'Please, James.' Her eyes were bright. 'Go and get on to him. He hasn't talked to you for weeks. Perhaps it's something important. Something exciting.' She tried desperately to put encouragement into her voice.

'It's always exciting starting a new life. Anyway, who's afraid of the Big Bad M.? Will you come and lend a hand on my chicken farm?'

She turned away and put her hands up to her face. He patted her casually on the shoulder and walked through into his office and went over and picked up the red telephone. '007 here, sir.'

'I'm sorry, sir. Had to go to the dentist.'

'I know, sir. I'm sorry. I left it in my desk.'

'Yes, sir.'

He put the receiver down slowly. He looked round his office as if saying goodbye to it, walked out and along the corridor and went up in the lift with the resignation of a man under sentence.

Miss Moneypenny looked up at him with ill-concealed hostility. 'You can go in.'

Bond squared his shoulders and looked at the padded door behind which he had so often heard his fate pronounced. Almost as if it were going to give him an electric shock, he tentatively reached out for the door handle and walked through and closed the door behind him.

3

THE IMPOSSIBLE MISSION

M., HIS shoulders hunched inside the square-cut blue suit, was standing by the big window looking out across the park. Without looking round he said, 'Sit down.' No name, no number!

Bond took his usual place across the desk from M.'s tall-armed chair. He noticed that there was no file on the expanse of red leather in front of the chair. And the In and Out baskets were both empty. Suddenly he felt really bad about every-thing – about letting M. down, letting the Service down, letting himself down. This empty desk, the empty chair, were the final accusation. We have nothing for you, they seemed to say. You're no use to us any more. Sorry. It's been nice know-ing you, but there it is.

M. came over and sat heavily down in the chair and looked across at Bond. There was nothing to read in the lined sailor's face. It was as impassive as the polished blue leather of the empty chairback had been.

M. said, 'You know why I've sent for you?'

'I can guess, sir. You can have my resignation.'

M. said angrily, 'What in hell are you talking about? It's not your fault that the Double-O Section's been idle for so long. It's the way things go. You've had flat periods before now – months with nothing in your line.'

'But I made a mess of the last two jobs. And I know my Medical's been pretty poor these last few months.'

'Nonsense. There's nothing the matter with you. You've been through a bad time. You've had good reason to be a bit under the weather. As for the last two assignments, anyone can make mistakes. But I can't have idle hands around the place, so I'm taking you out of the Double-O Section.'

Bond's heart had temporarily risen. Now it plummeted

again. The old man was being kind, trying to let him down lightly. He said, 'Then, if it's all the same to you, sir, I'd still like to put in my resignation. I've held the Double-O number for too long. I'm not interested in staff work, I'm afraid, sir. And no good at it either.'

M. did something Bond had never seen him do before. He lifted his right fist and brought it crashing down on the desk. 'Who the devil do you think you're talking to? Who the devil d'you think's running this show? God in Heaven! I send for you to give you promotion and the most important job of your career and you talk to me about resignation! Pig-headed young fool!'

Bond was dumbfounded. A great surge of excitement ran through him. What in hell was all this about? He said, 'I'm terribly sorry, sir. I thought I'd been letting the side down lately.'

'I'll soon tell you when you're letting the side down.' M. thumped the desk for a second time, but less hard. 'Now listen to me, I'm giving you acting promotion to the Diplomatic Section. Four figure number and a thousand a year extra pay. You won't know much about the Section, but I can tell you there are only two other men in it. You can keep your present office and your secretary, if you like. In fact I would prefer it. I don't want your change of duty to get about. Understand?'

'Yes, sir.'

'In any case, you'll be leaving for Japan inside a week. The Chief of Staff is handling the arrangements personally. Not even my secretary knows about it. As you can see,' M. waved his hand, 'there's not even a file on the case. That's how important it is.'

'But why have you chosen me, sir?' Bond's heart was thumping. This was the most extraordinary change in his fortunes that had ever come about! Ten minutes before he had been on the rubbish heap, his career, his life in ruins, and now here he was being set up on a pinnacle! What the hell was it all about?

'For the simple reason that the job's impossible. No, I won't go as far as that. Let's say totally improbable of success.

You've shown in the past that you have an aptitude for difficult assignments. The only difference here is that there won't
be any strong-arm stuff,' M. gave a frosty smile, 'none of the
gun-play you pride yourself on so much. It'll just be a question
of your wits and nothing else. But if you bring it off, which I
very much doubt, you will just about double our intelligence
about the Soviet Union.'

'Can you tell me some more about it, sir?'

'Have to, as there's nothing written down. Lower echelon
stuff, about the Japanese Secret Service and so forth, you can
get from Section J. The Chief of Staff will tell Colonel Hamilton to answer your questions freely, though you will tell him
nothing about the purpose of your mission. Understood?'

'Yes, sir.'

'Well now. You know a bit about cryptography?'

'The bare bones, sir. I've preferred to keep clear of the
subject. Better that way in case the Opposition ever got hold
of me.'

'Quite right. Well now, the Japanese are past masters at it.
They've got the right mentality for finicky problems in letters
and numbers. Since the war, under CIA guidance, they've built
incredible cracking machines – far ahead of IBM and so forth.
And for the last year they've been reading the cream of the
Soviet traffic from Vladivostok and Oriental Russia – diplomatic, naval, air-force, the lot.'

'That's terrific, sir.'

'Terrific for the CIA.'

'Aren't they passing it on to us, sir? I thought we were hand
in glove with CIA all along the line.'

'Not in the Pacific. They regard that as their private pre-
serve. When Allan Dulles was in charge, we used at least to
get digests of any stuff that concerned us, but this new man
McCone has cracked down on all that. He's a good man, all
right, and we get along well personally, but he's told me can-
didly that he's acting under orders – National Defence Coun-
cil. They're worried about our security. Can't blame them.
I'm equally worried about theirs. Two of their top crypto-
graphers defected a couple of years ago and they must have

blown a lot of the stuff we give the Americans. Trouble with this so-called democracy of ours is that the Press get hold of these cases and write them up too big. *Pravda* doesn't burst into tears when one of their men come over to us. *Izvestia* doesn't ask for a public inquiry. Somebody in K G B gets hell, I suppose. But at least they're allowed to get on with their job instead of having retired members of the Supreme Soviet pawing through their files and telling them how to run a secret service.'

Bond knew that M. had tendered his resignation after the Prenderghast case. This had involved a Head of Station with homosexual tendencies who had recently, amidst world-wide publicity, been given thirty years for treason. Bond himself had had to give evidence in that particular case, and he knew that the Questions in the House, the case at the Old Bailey, and the hearings before the Farrer Tribunal on the Intelligence Services that had followed, had held up all work at Headquarters for at least a month and brought about the suicide of a totally innocent Head of Section who had taken the whole affair as a direct reflection on his own probity. To get M. back on the track, Bond said, 'About this stuff the Japanese are getting. Where do I come in, sir?'

M. put both hands flat on the table. It was the old gesture when he came to the 64-dollar question, and Bond's heart lifted even further at the sight of it. 'There's a man in Tokyo called Tiger Tanaka. Head of their Secret Service. Can't remember what they call it. Some unpronounceable Japanese rubbish. He's quite a man. First at Oxford. Came back here and spied for them before the war. Joined the Kempeitai, their wartime Gestapo, trained as a *kami-kaze* and would be dead by now but for the surrender. Well, he's the chap who has control of the stuff we want, I want, the Chiefs of Staff want. You're to go out there and get it off him. How, I don't know. That's up to you. But you can see why I say you're unlikely to succeed. He's in fief' – Bond was amused by the old Scottish expression – 'to the C I A. He probably doesn't think much of us.' M.'s mouth bent down at the corners. 'People don't these days. They may be right or wrong. I'm not a politician. He doesn't know much about the Service except what he's penetrated or heard from the CIA. And that won't be greatly to our advantage, I'd say. We haven't had a Station in Japan since 1950. No traffic. It all went to the Americans. You'll be working under the Australians. They tell me their man's good. Section J says so too. Anyway, that's the way it is. If anyone can bring it off, you can. Care to have a try, James?'

M.'s face was suddenly friendly. It wasn't friendly often. James Bond felt a quick warmth of affection for this man who had ordered his destiny for so long, but whom he knew so little. His instinct told him that there were things hidden behind this assignment, motives which he didn't understand. Was this a rescue job on him? Was M. giving him his last chance? But it sounded solid enough. The reasons for it stood up. Hopeless? Impossible? Perhaps. Why hadn't M. chosen a Jap speaker? Bond had never been east of Hongkong. But then Orientalists had their own particular drawbacks – too much tied up with tea ceremonies and flower arrangements and Zen and so forth. No. It sounded a true bill. He said, 'Yes, sir. I'd like to have a try.'

M. gave an abrupt nod. 'Good.' He leant forward and pressed a button on the intercom. 'Chief of Staff? What number have you allotted to 007? Right. He's coming to see you straight away.'

M. leant back. He gave one of his rare smiles. 'You're stuck with your old digit. All right, four sevens. Go along and get briefed.'

Bond said, 'Right, sir. And, er, thank you.' He got up and walked over to the door and let himself out. He walked straight over to Miss Moneypenny and bent down and kissed her on the cheek. She turned pink and put a hand up to where he had kissed her. Bond said, 'Be an angel, Penny, and ring down to Mary and tell her she's got to get out of whatever she's doing tonight. I'm taking her out to dinner. Scotts. Tell her we'll have our first roast grouse of the year and pink champagne. Celebration.'

'What of?' Miss Moneypenny's eyes were suddenly wide and excited.

'Oh I don't know. The Queen's birthday or something. Right?' James Bond crossed the room and went into the Chief of Staff's office.

Miss Moneypenny picked up the inter-office telephone and passed on the message in a thrilled voice. She said, 'I do think he's all right again, Mary. It's all there again like it used to be. Heaven knows what M.'s been saying to him. He had lunch with Sir James Molony today. Don't tell James that. But it may have something to do with it. He's with the Chief of Staff now. And Bill said he wasn't to be disturbed. Sounds like some kind of a job. Bill was very mysterious.'

Bill Tanner, late Colonel Tanner of the Sappers and Bond's best friend in the Service, looked up from his heavily laden desk. He grinned with pleasure at what he saw. He said, 'Take a pew, James. So you've bought it? Thought you might. But it's a stinker all right. Think you can bring it off?'

'Not an earthly, I'd guess,' said Bond cheerfully. 'This man Tanaka sounds a tough nut, and I'm no great hand at diplomacy. But why did M. pick on me, Bill? I thought I was in the dog house because of messing up those last two jobs. I was all set to go into chicken farming. Now, be a good chap and tell me what's the real score.'

Bill Tanner had been ready for that one. He said easily, 'Balls, James. You've been running through a bad patch. We all hit 'em sometimes. M. just thought you'd be the best man for the job. You know he's got an entirely misplaced opinion of your abilities. Anyway, it'll be a change from your usual rough-housing. Time you moved up out of that damned Double-O Section of yours. Don't you ever think about promotion?'

'Absolutely not,' said Bond with fervour. 'As soon as I get back from this caper, I'll ask for my old number back again. But tell me, how am I supposed to set about this business? What's this Australian cover consist of? Have I got anything to offer this wily Oriental in exchange for his jewels? How's the stuff to be transmitted back here if I do get my hands on it? Must be the hell of a lot of traffic.'

'He can have the entire product of Station H. He can send

one of his own staffers down to Hongkong to sit in with us if he likes. He'll probably be pretty well off on China already, but he won't have anything as high grade as our Macao link, the "Blue Route". Hamilton will tell you all about that. In Tokyo, the man you'll be working with is an Aussie called Henderson – Richard Lovelace Henderson. Fancy name, but Section J and all the old Jap hands say he's a good man. You'll have an Australian passport and we'll fix for you to go out as his number two. That'll give you diplomatic status and a certain amount of face, which counts for damn near everything out there according to Hamilton. If you get the stuff, Henderson will push it back to us through Melbourne. We'll give him a communications staff to handle it. Next question.'

'What are the CIA going to say about all this? After all, it's bare-faced poaching.'

'They don't own Japan. Anyway, they're not to know. That's up to this fellow Tanaka. He'll have to fix the machinery for getting it into the Australian Embassy. That's his worry. But the whole thing's on pretty thin ice. The main problem is to make sure he doesn't go straight along to the CIA and tell 'em of your approach. If you get blown, we'll just have to get the Australians to hold the baby. They've done it before when we've been bowled out edging our way into the Pacific. We're good friends with their Service. First-rate bunch of chaps. And, anyway, the CIA's hands aren't as clean as all that. We've got a whole file of cases where they've crossed wires with us round the world. Often dangerously. We can throw that book at McCone if this business blows up in our faces. But part of your job is to see that it doesn't.'

'Seems to me I'm getting all balled up in high politics. Not my line of country at all. But is this stuff really as vital as M. says?'

'Absolutely. If you get hold of it, your grateful country will probably buy you that chicken farm you're always talking about.'

'So be it. Now, if you'll give Hamilton a buzz I'll go and start learning all about the mysterious East.'

'*Kangei!* Welcome aboard,' said the pretty kimono-ed and

obi-ed stewardess of Japan Air Lines as, a week later, James
Bond settled into the comfortable window seat of the four-jet,
turbofan Douglas DC8 at London Airport and listened to the
torrent of soft Japanese coming from the tannoy that would
be saying all those things about life jackets and the flying time
to Orly. The sick-bags 'in case of motion disturbance' were
embellished with pretty bamboo emblems and, according to
the exquisitely bound travel folder, the random scribbles on
the luggage rack above his head were 'the traditional and
auspicious tortoiseshell motif'. The stewardess bowed and
handed him a dainty fan, a small hot towel in a wicker-basket
and a sumptuous menu that included a note to the effect that
an assortment of cigarettes, perfumes and pearls were available for sale. Then they were off with 50,000 pounds of thrust
on the first leg of the four that would take the good aircraft
Yoshino over the North Pole to Tokyo.

Bond gazed at the picture of three oranges (no! after an
hour he decided they were persimmons) in a blue bowl that
faced him and, when the aircraft flattened out at 30,000 feet,
ordered the first of the chain of brandies and ginger ales that
was to sustain him over the Channel, a leg of the North Sea,
the Kattegat, the Arctic Ocean, the Beaufort Sea, the Bering
Sea and the North Pacific Ocean and decided that, whatever
happened on this impossible assignment, he would put up no
resistance to his old skin being sloughed off him on the other
side of the world. By the time he was admiring the huge
stuffed Polar bear at Anchorage, in Alaska, the embrace of
JAL's soft wings had persuaded him that he didn't even mind
if the colour of the new skin was to be yellow.

4

DIKKO ON THE GINZA

THE huge right fist crashed into the left palm with the noise
of a .45 pistol shot. The great square face of the Australian
turned almost purple and the veins stood out on the grizzled

temples. With controlled violence, but almost under his breath, he intoned savagely:

> 'I bludge,
> Thou bludgest,
> He bludges,
> We bludge,
> You bludge,
> They all bludge.'

He reached under the low table and then seemed to think better of it and moved his hand to the glass of *sake*, picked it up and poured it down his throat without a swallow.

Bond said mildly, 'Take it easy, Dikko. What's bitten you? And what does this vulgar-sounding colonial expression mean?'

Richard Lovelace Henderson, of Her Majesty's Australian Diplomatic Corps, looked belligerently round the small crowded bar in a by-street off the Ginza and said out of the corner of his large and usually cheerful mouth that was now turned down in bitterness and anger, 'You stupid pommy bastard, we've been miked! That bludger Tanaka's miked us! Here, under the table! See the little wire down the leg? And see that wingy over at the bar? Chap with one arm looking bloody respectable in his blue suit and black tie? That's one of Tiger's men. I can smell 'em by now. They've been tailing me off and on for ten years. Tiger dresses 'em all like little CIA gentlemen. You watch out for any Jap who's drinking Western and wearing that rig. All Tiger's men.' He grumbled, 'Damn good mind to go over and call the bastard.'

Bond said, 'Well, if we're being miked, all this'll make sweet reading for Mr Tanaka tomorrow morning.'

'What the hell,' said Dikko Henderson resignedly. 'The old bastard knows what I think of him. Now he'll just have it in writing. Teach him to stop leaning on me. And my friends,' he added, with a blistering glance at Bond. 'It's really you he wants to size up. And I don't mind if he hears me saying so. Bludger? Well, hear me now, Tiger! This is the great Australian insult. You can use it anyways.' He raised his voice. 'But in general it means a worthless pervert, ponce, scoundrel, liar, traitor and rogue – with no redeeming feature. And I hope your stewed seaweed sticks in your gullet at breakfast tomorrow when you know what I think of you.'

Bond laughed. The torrent of powerful swear-words had started its ceaseless flow the day before at the airport – Haneda, 'the field of wings'. It had taken Bond nearly an hour to extract his single suitcase from the customs area, and he had emerged fuming into the central hall only to be jostled and pushed aside by an excited crowd of young Japanese bearing paper banners that said 'International Laundry Convention'. Bond was exhausted from his flight. He let out one single four-letter expletive.

Behind him a big voice repeated the same word and added some more. 'That's my boy! That's the right way to greet the East! You'll be needing all those words and more before you're through with the area.'

Bond had turned. The huge man in the rumpled grey suit thrust out a hand as big as a small ham. 'Glad to meet you. I'm Henderson. As you were the only pommy on the plane, I guess you're Bond. Here. Give me that bag. Got a car outside and the sooner we get away from this blankety blank madhouse the better.'

Henderson looked like a middle-aged prize fighter who has retired and taken to the bottle. His thin suit bulged with muscle round the arms and shoulders and with fat round the waist. He had a craggy, sympathetic face, rather stony blue eyes, and a badly broken nose. He was sweating freely (Bond was to find that he was always sweating), and as he barged his way through the crowd, using Bond's suitcase as a battering ram, he extracted a rumpled square of terry cloth from his trouser-pocket and wiped it round his neck and face. The crowd parted unresentfully to let the giant through, and Bond followed in his wake to a smart Toyopet saloon waiting in a no-parking area. The chauffeur got out and bowed. Henderson fired a torrent of instructions at him in fluent Japanese and followed Bond into the back seat, settling himself with a grunt. 'Taking you to your hotel first – the Okura, latest of the

Western ones. American tourist got murdered at the Royal
Oriental the other day and we don't want to lose you all that
soon. Then we'll do a bit of serious drinking. Had some
dinner?'

'About six of them, as far as I can remember. JAL certainly
takes good care of your stomach.'

'Why did you choose the willow-pattern route? How was
the old ruptured duck?'

'They told me the bird was a crane. Very dainty. But efficient. Thought I might as well practise being inscrutable before
plunging into all this.' Bond waved at the cluttered shambles
of the Tokyo suburbs through which they were tearing at
what seemed to Bond a suicidal speed. 'Doesn't look the most
attractive city in the world. And why are we driving on the
left?'

'God knows,' said Henderson moodily. 'The bloody Japs
do everything the wrong way round. Read the old instruction
books wrong, I daresay. Light switches go up instead of down.
Taps turn to the left. Door handles likewise. Why, they even
race their horses clockwise instead of anti-clockwise like
civilized people. As for Tokyo, it's bloody awful. It's either
too hot or too cold or pouring with rain. And there's an earth-
quake about every day. But don't worry about them. They
just make you feel slightly drunk. The typhoons are worse. If
one starts to blow, go into the stoutest bar you can see and get
drunk. But the first ten years are the worst. It's got its point
when you know your way around. Bloody expensive if you live
Western, but I stick to the back alleys and do all right. Really
quite exhilarating. Got to know the lingo though, and when
to bow and take off your shoes and so on. You'll have to get
the basic routines straight pretty quickly if you're going to
make any headway with the people you've come to see. Under-
neath the stiff collars and striped pants in the government
departments, there's still plenty of the old *samurai* tucked
away. I laugh at them for it, and they laugh back because
they've got to know my line of patter. But that doesn't mean I
don't bow from the waist when I know it's expected of me and
when I want something. You'll get the hang of it all right.'

Henderson fired some Japanese at the driver who had been glancing frequently in his driving mirror. The driver laughed and replied cheerfully. 'Thought so,' said Henderson. 'We've got ourselves a tail. Typical of old Tiger. I told him you were staying at the Okura, but he wants to make sure for himself. Don't worry. It's just part of his crafty ways. If you find one of his men breathing down your neck in bed tonight, or a girl if you're lucky, just talk to them politely and they'll bow and hiss themselves out.'

But a solitary sleep had followed the serious drinking in the Bamboo Bar of the Okura, and the next day had been spent doing the sights and getting some cards printed that described Bond as Second Secretary in the Cultural Department of the Australian Embassy. 'They know that's our intelligence side,' said Henderson, 'and they know I'm the head of it and you're my temporary assistant, so why not spell it out for them?' And that evening they had gone for more serious drinking to Henderson's favourite bar, Melody's, off the Ginza, where everybody called Henderson 'Dikko' or 'Dikko-san', and where they were ushered respectfully to the quiet corner table that appeared to be his *Stammtisch*.

And now Henderson reached under the table and, with a powerful wrench, pulled out the wires and left them hanging. 'I'll give that black bastard Melody hell for this when I get around to it,' he said belligerently. 'And to think of all I've done for the dingo bastard! Used to be a favourite pub of the English Colony and the Press Club layabouts. Had a good restaurant attached to it. That's gone now. The Eyeteye cook trod on the cat and spilled the soup and he picked up the cat and threw it into the cooking stove. Of course that got around pretty quick, and all the animal-lovers and sanctimonious bastards got together and tried to have Melody's licence taken away. I managed to put in squeeze in the right quarter and saved him, but everyone quit his restaurant and he had to close it. I'm the only regular who's stuck to him. And now he goes and does this to me! Oh well, he'll have had the squeeze put on *him*, I suppose. Anyway, that's the end of the tape so far as T.T.'s concerned. I'll give him hell too. He ought to have

learned by now that me and my friends don't want to assassinate the Emperor or blow up the Diet or something.' Dikko
glared around him as if he proposed to do both those things.
'Now then, James, to business. I've fixed up for you to meet
Tiger tomorrow morning at eleven. I'll pick you up and
take you there. "The Bureau of All-Asian Folkways." I
won't describe it to you. It'd spoil it. Now, I don't really know
what you're here for. Spate of top secret cables from Melbourne. To be deciphered by yours truly in person. Thanks
very much! And my Ambassador, Jim Saunderson, good
bloke, says he doesn't want to know anything about it. Thinks
it'd be even better if he didn't meet you at all. Okay with you?
No offence, but he's a wise guy and likes to keep his hands
clean. And I don't want to know anything about your job
either. That way, you're the only one who gets the powdered
bamboo in his coffee. But I gather you want to get some high-
powered gen out of Tiger without the CIA knowing anything about it. Right? Well that's going to be a dicey business.
Tiger's a career man with a career mind. Although, on the
surface, he's a hundred per cent *demokorasu,* he's a deep one –
very deep indeed. The American occupation and the American
influence here look like a very solid basis for a total American-
Japanese alliance. But once a Jap, always a Jap. It's the same
with all the other great nations – Chinese, Russian, German,
English. It's their bones that matter, not their lying faces. And
all those races have got tremendous bones. Compared with the
bones, the smiles or scowls don't mean a thing. And time
means nothing for them either. Ten years is the blink of a star
for the big ones. Get me? So Tiger, and his superiors, who, I
suppose, are the Diet and, in the end, the Emperor, will look at
your proposition principally from two angles. Is it immediately desirable, today? Or is it a long-term investment? Something that may pay off for the country in ten, twenty years.
And, if I were you, I'd stick to that spiel – the long-term talk.
These people, people like Tiger, who's an absolutely top man
in Japan, don't think in terms of days or months or years. They
think in terms of centuries. Quite right, when you come to
think of it.'

Dikko Henderson made a wide gesture with his left hand. Bond decided that Dikko was getting cheerfully tight. He had found a Palomar pony to run with. They must be rare enough in Tokyo. They were both past the eighth flask of *sake*, but Dikko had also laid a foundation of Suntory whisky in the Okura while he'd been waiting for Bond to write out an innocuous cable to Melbourne with the prefix 'Information-wise', which meant that it was for Mary Goodnight, to announce his arrival and give his current address. But it was all right with Bond that Dikko should be getting plastered. He would talk better and looser and, in the end, wiser that way. And Bond wanted to pick his brains.

Bond said, 'But what sort of a chap is this Tanaka? Is he your enemy or your friend?'

'Both. More of a friend probably. At least I'd guess so. I amuse him. His CIA pals don't. He loosens up with me. We've got things in common. We share a pleasure in the delights of *samsara* – wine and women. He's a great cocks-man. I also have ambitions in that direction. I've managed to keep him out of two marriages. Trouble with Tiger is he always wants to marry 'em. He's paying cock-tax, that's alimony in the Australian vernacular, to three already. So he's acquired an ON with regard to me. That's an obligation – almost as important in the Japanese way of life as "face". When you have an ON, you're not very happy until you've discharged it honourably, if you'll pardon the bad pun. And if a man makes you a present of a salmon, you mustn't repay him with a shrimp. It's got to be with an equally large salmon – larger if possible, so that then you've jumped the man, and now he has an ON with regard to you, and you're quids in morally, socially and spiritually – and the last one's the most important. Well now. Tiger's ON towards me is a very powerful one, very difficult to discharge. He's paid little slices of it off with various intelligence dope. He's paid off another big slice by accepting your presence here and giving you an interview so soon after your arrival. If you'd been an ordinary supplicant, it might have taken you weeks. He'd have given you a fat dose of *shikiri-naoshi* – that's making you wait, giving you the great

stone face. The *sumo* wrestlers use it in the ring to make an opponent look and feel small in front of the audience. Got it? So
you start with that in your favour. He would be predisposed to
do what you want because that would remove all his ON towards me and, by his accounting, stick a whole packet of
ON on my back towards him. But it's not so simple as that.
All Japanese have permanent ON towards their superiors, the
Emperor, their ancestors and the Japanese gods. This they can
only discharge by doing "the right thing". Not easy, you'll
say. Because how can you know what the higher echelon
thinks is the right thing? Well, you get out of that by doing
what the bottom of the ladder thinks right – i.e. your immediate superiors. That passes the buck, psychologically, on to the
Emperor, and he's got to make his peace with ancestors and
gods. But that's all right with him, because he embodies all the
echelons above him, so he can get on with dissecting fish,
which is his hobby, with a clear conscience. Got it? It's not
really as mysterious as it sounds. Much the same routine as
operates in big corporations, like ICI or Shell, or in the Services, except with them the ladder stops at the Board of Direc-
tors or the Chiefs of Staff. It's easier that way. You don't have
to involve the Almighty and your great-grandfather in a decision to cut the price of aspirin by a penny a bottle.'

'It doesn't sound very *demokorasu* to me.'

'Of course it isn't, you dumb bastard. For God's sake, get it
into your head that the Japanese are a separate human species.
They've only been operating as a civilized people, in the debased sense we talk about it in the West, for fifty, at the most a
hundred years. Scratch a Russian and you'll find a Tartar.
Scratch a Japanese and you'll find a *samurai* – or what he thinks
is a *samurai*. Most of this *samurai* stuff is a myth, like the Wild
West bunk the Americans are brought up on, or your knights
in shining armour at King Arthur's court. Just because people
play baseball and wear bowler hats doesn't mean they're quote
civilized unquote. Just to show you I'm getting rather tight –
not drunk, mark you – I'd add that the UN are going to reap
the father and mother of a whirlwind by quote liberating unquote the colonial peoples. Give 'em a thousand years, yes.

But give 'em ten, no. You're only taking away their blow-pipes and giving them machine guns. Just you wait for the first one to start crying to high heaven for nuclear fission. Because they must have quote parity unquote with the lousy colonial powers. I'll give you ten years for that to happen, my friend. And when it does, I'll dig myself a deep hole in the ground and sit in it.'

Bond laughed. 'That also doesn't sound very *demokorasu*.'

' "I fornicate upon thy *demokorasu*" as brother Hemingway would have said. I stand for government by an *élite*.' Dikko Henderson downed his ninth pint of *sake*. 'And voting graded by each individual's rating in that *élite*. And one tenth of a vote for my government if you don't agree with me!'

'For God's sake, Dikko! How in hell did we get on to politics? Let's go and get some food. I'll agree there's a certain aboriginal common sense in what you say. . . . '

'Don't talk to me about the aborigines! What in hell do you think you know about the aborigines? Do you know that in my country there's a move afoot, not afoot, at full gallop, to give the aborigines the vote? You pommy poofter. You give me any more of that liberal crap and I'll have your balls for a bow-tie.'

Bond said mildly, 'What's a poofter?'

'What you'd call a pansy. No,' Dikko Henderson got to his feet and fired a string of what sounded like lucid Japanese at the man behind the bar, 'before I condemn you utterly, we'll go and eat eels – place where you can get a serious bottle of plonk to match. Then we'll go to "The House of Total Delight". After that, I will give you my honest verdict, honestly come by.'

Bond said, 'You're a no-good kangaroo bum, Dikko. But I like eels. As long as they're not jellied. I'll pay for them and for the later relaxation. You pay for the rice wine and the plonk, whatever that is. Take it easy. The wingy at the bar has an appraising look.'

'I come to appraise Mr Richard Lovelace Henderson, not to bury him.' Dikko Henderson produced a wad of thousand yen notes and began counting them out for the waiter. 'Not yet, that is.' He walked, with careful majesty, up to the bar and addressed himself to the large Negro in a plum-coloured coat behind it. 'Melody, be ashamed of yourself!' Then he led the way, with massive dignity, out of the bar.

5

MAGIC 44

DIKKO HENDERSON came to fetch Bond at ten o'clock next morning. He was considerably overhung. The hard blue eyes were veined with blood and he made straight for the Bamboo Bar and ordered himself a double brandy and ginger ale. Bond said mildly, 'You shouldn't have poured all that *sake* on top of the Suntory. I can't believe Japanese whisky makes a good foundation for anything.'

'You've got something there, sport. I've got myself a proper *futsukayoi* – honourable hangover. Mouth like a vulture's crutch. Soon as we got home from that lousy cat house, I had to go for the big spit. But you're wrong about Suntory. It's a good enough brew. Stick to the cheapest, the White Label, at around fifteen bob a bottle. There are two smarter brands, but the cheap one's the best. Went up to the distillery some whiles ago and met one of the family. Told me an interesting thing about whisky. He said you can only make good whisky where you can take good photographs. Ever heard that one? Said it was something to do with the effect of clear light on the alcohol. But did I talk a lot of crap last night? Or did you? Seem to recollect that one of us did.'

'You only gave me hell about the state of the world and called me a poofter. But you were quite friendly about it. No offence given or taken.'

'Oh, Christ!' Dikko Henderson gloomily pushed a hand through his tough, grizzled hair. 'But I didn't hit anyone?'

'Only that girl you slapped so hard on the bottom that she fell down.'

'Oh that!' said Dikko Henderson with relief. 'That was just a love-pat. What's a girl's bottom for, anyway? And so far as I recall they all screamed with laughter. Including her. Right? How did you make out with yours by the way? She looked pretty enthusiastic.'

'She was.'

'Good show.' He swallowed the remains of his drink and got to his feet. 'Come on, bud. Let's go. Wouldn't do to keep Tiger waiting. I once did and he wouldn't speak to me for a week.'

It was a typical Tokyo day in late summer – hot, sticky and grey – the air full of fine dust from the endless demolition and reconstruction work. They drove for half an hour towards Yokohama and pulled up outside a dull grey building which announced itself in large letters to be 'The Bureau of All-Asian Folkways'. There was a busy traffic of Japanese scurrying in and out through the bogusly important-looking entrance, but no one glanced at Dikko and Bond, and they were not asked their business as Dikko led the way through an entrance hall where there were books and postcards on sale as if the place were some kind of museum. Dikko made for a doorway marked 'Coordination Department' and there was a long corridor with open rooms on both sides. The rooms were full of studious-looking young men at desks. There were large wall maps with coloured pins dotted across them, and endless shelves of books. A door marked 'International Relations' gave on to another corridor, this time lined with closed doors which had people's names on them in English and Japanese. A sharp right turn took them through the 'Visual Presentation Bureau' with more closed doors, and on to 'Documentation', a large hall-shaped library with more people bent over desks. Here, for the first time, they were scrutinized by a man at a desk near the entrance. He rose to his feet and bowed wordlessly. As they walked on Dikko said quietly, 'This is where the cover tapers off. Up till now, all those people really were researching Asian Folkways. But these here are part of Tiger's outside staff, doing more or less classified work. Sort of archivists. This is where we'd be politely turned back if we'd lost our way.' Behind a final wall of bookshelves that stretched out into the room a small door was concealed. It was marked 'Proposed Extension to Documentation Department. Danger! Construction work in progress'. From behind it came the sound of drills, a circular saw cutting through the wood and other building noises. Dikko walked through the door into a totally empty room with a highly-polished wood floor. There was no sign of construction work. Dikko laughed at Bond's surprise. He gestured towards a large metal box fitted to the back of the door through which they had come. 'Tape recorder,' he said. 'Clever gimmick. Sounds just like the real thing. And this' – he pointed to the stretch of bare floor ahead – 'is what the Japanese call a "nightingale floor". Relic of the old days when people wanted to be warned of intruders. Serves the same purpose here. Imagine trying to get across here without being heard.' They set off, and immediately the cunningly sprung boards gave out penetrating squeaks and groans. In a small facing door, a spy-hole slid open and one large eye surveyed them. The door opened to reveal a stocky man in plain clothes who had been sitting at a small deal table reading a book. It was a tiny box-like room that seemed to have no other exit. The man bowed. Dikko said some phrases containing the words 'Tanaka-san'. The man bowed again. Dikko turned to Bond. 'You're on your own now. Be in it, champ! Tiger'll send you back to your hotel. See you.'

Bond said, 'Tell Mother I died game,' and walked into the little box and the door was closed behind him. There was a row of buttons by the desk and the guard pressed one of them. There came a barely perceptible whine and Bond got the impression of descent. So the room was a lift. What a box of tricks the formidable Tiger had erected as a screen for himself! The authentic Eastern nest of boxes. What next?

The descent continued for some time. When it stopped, the guard opened the door and Bond stepped out and stood stock still. He was standing on the platform of an underground station! There it all was: the red and green signals over the two yawning tunnels, the conventional white tiles on the walls and the curved roof – even an empty cigarette kiosk let into the wall beside him! A man had come out of this. He now said in good English, 'Please to follow me, Commander,' and led the way through an arch marked 'Exit'. But here all the floor space of the hall that would one day lead to the moving stairways was occupied by trim prefabricated offices on both sides of a wide corridor. Bond was led into the first of these which revealed itself as a waiting-room and outer office. A male secretary rose from his typewriter, bowed and went through a communicating door. He immediately reappeared, bowed again and held the door open. 'Please to come this way, Commander.'

Bond went through and the door was softly closed behind him. The big square figure that Dikko had described to him came forward across the handsome red carpet and held out a hand that was hard and dry. 'My dear Commander. Good morning. It is a great pleasure to meet you.' The wide, gold-toothed smile signalled welcome. The eyes glittered between long dark lashes that were almost feminine. 'Come and sit down. How do you like my offices? Rather different from your own Chief's, no doubt. But the new underground will take another ten years to complete and there is little office space in Tokyo. It crossed my mind to make use of this disused station. It is quiet. It is private. It is also cool. I shall be sorry when the trains are required to run and we shall have to move out.'

Bond took the proffered chair across the empty desk from Tanaka. 'It's a brilliant idea. And I enjoyed the Folkways above our heads. Are there really so many people in the world interested in Folkways?'

Tiger Tanaka shrugged. 'What does it matter? The literature is given away free. I have never asked the Director who reads it. Americans, I expect, and Germans. Perhaps some Swiss. The serious-minded can always be found for such stuff. It is an expensive conceit, of course. But fortunately the expense is not carried by the Ministry of Internal Affairs with whom I am concerned. Down here, we have to count our pennies. I suppose it is the same with your own budget.'

Bond assumed that this man would know the published facts of the Secret Service Vote. He said, 'Under ten million pounds a year doesn't go far when there is the whole world to cover.'

The teeth glistened under the neon strip lighting. 'At least for the last ten years you have saved money by closing down your activities in this part of the world.'

'Yes. We rely on the CIA to do our work here for us. They are most efficient and helpful.'

'As much so under McCone as under Dulles?'

The old fox! 'Nearly so. Nowadays they are even more inclined to regard the Pacific as their own back garden.'

'From which you wish to borrow the mowing machine. Without them knowing.' Tiger's smile was even more tigerish.

Bond had to laugh. The wily devil had certainly been putting two and two together. When Bond laughed, Tiger also laughed, but carefully. Bond said, 'We had a man called Captain Cook and various others who discovered much of this garden. Australia and New Zealand are two very great countries. You must admit that our interest in this half of the world is perfectly legitimate.'

'My dear Commander. You were lucky that we struck at Pearl Harbour rather than at Australia. Can you doubt that we would have occupied that country and New Zealand if we had done otherwise? These are big and important land spaces, insufficiently developed. You could not have defended them. The Americans would not have. If our policy had been different, we would now own half the British Commonwealth. Personally, I have never understood the strategy behind Pearl Harbour. Did we wish to conquer America? The supply lines were too long. But Australia and New Zealand were ripe for the plucking.' He pushed forward a large box of cigarettes. 'Do you smoke? These are Shinsei. It is an acceptable brand.'

James Bond was running out of his Morland specials. He would soon have to start on the local stuff. He also had to collect his thoughts. This was rather like being involved in a Summit meeting between the United Kingdom and Japan. He felt way out of his depth. He took a cigarette and lit it. It burned rapidly with something of the effect of a slow-burning firework. It had a vague taste of American blends, but it was good and sharp on the palate and lungs like 90 proof spirits. He let the smoke out in a quiet hiss and smiled. 'Mr Tanaka, these are matters for political historians. I am concerned with much lower matters. And matters concerning the future rather than the past.'

'I quite understand, Commander.' Tiger Tanaka was obviously displeased that his game of generalities had been dodged by Bond. 'But we have a saying "Speak of next year and the devil laughs". The future is inscrutable. But tell me, what are your impressions of Japan? You have been enjoying yourself?'

'I imagine that one always enjoys oneself with Dikko Henderson.'

'Yes, he is a man who lives as if he were going to die tomorrow. This is a correct way to live. He is a good friend of mine. I greatly enjoy his company. We have certain tastes in common.'

Bond said ironically, 'Folkways?'

'Exactly.'

'He has a great affection for you. I do not know him well, but I suspect that he is a lonely man. It is an unfortunate combination to be both lonely and intelligent. Wouldn't it be a good thing for him to marry a Japanese girl and settle down? Couldn't you find him one?' Bond was pleased that the conversation had descended to personalities. He sensed that he was on the right track. At least on a better track than this talk about power politics. But there would come a bad moment when he would have to get down to business. He didn't care for the prospect.

As if he had sensed this, Tiger Tanaka said, 'I have arranged for our friend to meet many Japanese girls. The result in every case has been negative, or, at the best, fleeting. But tell me, Commander. We have not met here to discuss Mr Henderson's private life. In what respect can I be of service to you? Is it the lawn mower?'

Bond smiled. 'It is. The manufacturers' trade mark for this particular implement is MAGIC 44.'

'Ah yes. A most valuable implement of many uses. I can understand that your country would wish to have the services of this implement. A case in point is an example of its capabilities which came into my hands only this morning.' Tiger Tanaka opened a drawer in his desk and extracted a file. It was a pale green file stamped in a square box with the word GOKUHI in black Japanese and Roman characters. Bond assumed this to be the equivalent of Top Secret. He put this to Mr Tanaka who confirmed it. Mr Tanaka opened the file and extracted two sheets of yellow paper. Bond could see that one was covered with Japanese ideograms and that the other had perhaps fifty lines of typewriting. Mr Tanaka slipped the typewritten one across the desk. He said, 'May I beg you on oath not to reveal to anyone what you are about to read?'

'If you insist, Mr Tanaka.'

'I am afraid I must, Commander.'

'So be it.' Bond drew the sheet of paper towards him. The text was in English. This is what it said:

TO ALL STATIONS OF GRADE TWO AND ABOVE. TO BE DECIPHERED BY ADDRESSEE PERSONALLY AND THEN DESTROYED. WHEN DESTRUCTION HAS BEEN EFFECTED CONFIRM BY THE CODE WORD QUOTE SATURN UNQUOTE. TEXT BEGINS: IN AMPLIFICATION OF NUMBER ONES PUBLISHED SPEECH TO THE SUPREME SOVIET ON SEPTEMBER FIRST THIS CONFIRMS THAT WE ARE IN POSSESSION OF THE TWO HUNDRED MEGATON WEAPON AND THAT A TEST FIRING WILL TAKE PLACE ON SEPTEMBER TWENTIETH AT HIGH ALTITUDE IN THE NOVAYA ZEMLYA AREA STOP CONSIDERABLE FALLOUT CAN BE EXPECTED AND PUBLIC OUTCRY CAN BE ANTICIPATED IN THE ARCTIC, NORTH PACIFIC AND ALASKAN AREAS STOP THIS SHOULD BE COUNTERED AND WILL BE COUNTERED FROM MOSCOW BY REFERENCE TO THE MORE RECENT TESTS BY AMERICA AND TO NUMBER ONES REPEATED DEMANDS FOR AN END TO TESTS OF NUCLEAR FISSION WEAPONS OF OFFENCE WHICH HAVE SUCCESSIVELY BEEN REBUFFED STOP FOR INFORMATION THE DELIVERY OF ONE SUCH WEAPON BY ICBM ON LONDON WOULD DESTROY ALL LIFE AND PROPERTY SOUTH OF A LINE DRAWN

BETWEEN NEWCASTLE AND CARLISLE STOP IT FOLLOWS THAT A
SECOND MISSILE DROPPED IN THE NEIGHBOURHOOD OF ABER-
DEEN WOULD INEVITABLY RESULT IN THE TOTAL DESTRUCTION
OF BRITAIN AND ALL IRELAND STOP THIS FACT WILL SHORTLY
BE EMPLOYED BY NUMBER ONE AS THE TEETH IN A DIPLOMATIC
DEMARCHE DESIGNED TO ACHIEVE THE REMOVAL OF ALL
AMERICAN BASES AND OFFENSIVE WEAPONS FROM BRITAIN
AND THE NUCLEAR DISARMAMENT OF BRITAIN ITSELF STOP
THIS WILL TEST TO THE UTTERMOST AND PROBABLY DESTROY
THE ANGLO HYPHEN AMERICAN ALLIANCE SINCE IT CAN BE
ASSUMED THAT AMERICA WILL NOT RISK A NUCLEAR WAR IN-
VOLVING HER TERRITORY FOR THE SAKE OF RESCUING A NOW
MORE OR LESS VALUELESS ALLY DASH AN ALLY NOW OPENLY
REGARDED IN WASHINGTON AS OF LITTLE MORE ACCOUNT
THAN BELGIUM OR ITALY STOP IF THIS DIPLOMATIC DEMARCHE
COMMA WHICH MUST OF COURSE BE CATEGORIZED AS CARRY-
ING SOME DEGREE OF RISK COMMA IS SUCCESSFUL IT FOLLOWS
THAT SIMILAR DEMARCHES WILL BE UNDERTAKEN IN EUROPE
AND LATER IN THE PACIFIC AREA COMMA INDIVIDUAL COUN-
TRIES BEING SINGLED OUT ONE BY ONE FOR TERRORIZATION
AND DEMORALIZATION STOP THE FINAL FRUITS OF THIS
GRAND STRATAGEM IF SUCCESSFUL WILL GUARANTEE THE
SECURITY OF THE USSR FOR THE FORESEEABLE FUTURE AND
ULTIMATELY RESULT IN PEACEFUL COEXISTENCE WITH
AMERICA STOP PEACEFUL INTENT OF THE USSR WILL THERE-
FORE BE EMPHASIZED THROUGHOUT BY NUMBER ONE AND BY
ALL GOVERNMENT AGENCIES STOP THIS LINE OF REASONING
YOU WILL ALSO FOLLOW SHOULD YOUR STATION BE AT ANY
TIME INVOLVED OR AFFECTED STOP INFORMATIVELY ALL
SOVIET CITIZENS WORKING IN BRITAIN WILL BE WITHDRAWN
FROM THAT COUNTRY ONE WEEK BEFORE THE INITIAL DE-
MARCHE STOP NO EXPLANATION WILL BE GIVEN BUT A CON-
SIDERABLE AND DESIRABLE HEIGHTENING OF TENSION WILL
THUS BE ACHIEVED STOP THE SAME PROCEDURE WHICH CAN
BE CATEGORIZED AS A SOFTENING UP OF THE TARGET COUN-
TRY WILL BE FOLLOWED IN THE SECONDARY DEMARCHES RE-
FERRED TO ABOVE STOP FOR THE TIME BEING YOU SHOULD
TAKE NO PRECAUTIONARY STEPS ON YOUR STATION EXCEPT TO

PREPARE YOUR MIND IN TOTAL SECRECY FOR THE EVENTU-
ALITY THAT YOUR STATION MAY BECOME INVOLVED AT SOME
LATER DATE AND THAT EVACUATION OF YOUR STAFF AND THE
BURNING OF ARCHIVES WILL BECOME MANDATORY ON RE-
CEIPT OF THE CODE WORD QUOTE LIGHTNING UNQUOTE
ADDRESSED TO YOU PERSONALLY OVER CIRCUIT FORTY
HYPHEN FOUR STOP END OF TEXT SIGNED CENTRAL.

James Bond pushed the document away from him as if he
feared contamination from it. He let out his breath in a quiet
hiss. He reached for the box of Shinsei and lit one, drawing the
harsh smoke deep down into his lungs. He raised his eyes to
Mr Tanaka's, which were regarding him with polite interest.
'I suppose Number One is Khrushchev?'

'That is correct, and the meaning of stations grade two and
above is consulates general and embassies. It is interesting
material, is it not?'

'It is a mistake that you are keeping this material from us.
We have a treaty of friendship and a trade treaty with you. Do
you not regard the withholding of this vital information as a
dishonourable act?'

'Honour is a very serious word in Japan, Commander.
Would it not be even more dishonourable to break our word
to our good American friends? They have several times
assured me and my government that any information of vital
importance to our other friends and allies will be passed on to
them in such a way as not to divulge the source. I have no
evidence that they are not pursuing this routine.'

'You know as well as I do, Mr Tanaka, that rewriting and
doctoring to conceal the source reduces this type of material
to a grade no higher than secret reports from countless other
"delicate and reliable" sources. The nature of this particular
source, the fact that one is reading the very words of the
enemy, is at least fifty per cent of the value of the information
this message contains. No doubt Washington will pass on a
garbled version of this message to London. I hope they already
have. But you realize that it might be in their interests to keep
quiet about this terrible threat that hangs over England? At

the same time, it is in England's interest to use every hour in devising some counter to this plan. One small step, which at once comes to mind, is preparations for the internment of all Soviet citizens in Britain at the first sign of the evacuation measures mentioned in the message.'

'I appreciate your point of view, Commander. There is of course, in this instance, an alternative route for this information to reach your government.' Mr Tanaka's face crinkled wickedly.

Bond leant urgently over the desk. 'But I gave my word of honour!'

Mr Tanaka's face underwent a curious change. All the upward lines turned downwards. The dark eyes lost their glitter and assumed an inward look. In a curious way, the whole face slumped into melancholy. He said, 'Commander, I was very happy in England. Your people were very good to me. I repaid them in an unworthy fashion.' (Ah! thought Bond. The ON.) 'I plead youth and the heat of a war that I thought would bring much glory to my country. I was mistaken. We were defeated. The expiation of that dishonour is a large matter, a matter for the youth of this country. I am not a politician and I do not know what course that expiation will take. At present we are going through the usual transition period of the vanquished. But I, Tanaka, have my own private accounting to balance. I am in great debt to your country. This morning I have betrayed a State secret to you. I was encouraged in my action by my friendship for Dikko. I was also encouraged by the sincerity of your bearing and the honesty of your approach to the duty that has been laid upon you. I fully realize the importance of this piece of paper to Britain. You remember its contents?'

'Exactly, I think.'

'And you are on your honour not to communicate it elsewhere.'

'Yes.'

Tiger Tanaka got to his feet and held out his hand. 'Goodbye for the time being, Commander. I hope that we shall be seeing more of each other.' The powerful face lit up again.

Now there was no pretence in the great golden smile. 'Honour is a pattern of behaviour, Commander. The bamboo must bend to the breeze. But equally the cedar must bend to the typhoon. The meaning of this is that sometimes duty is more compelling than any words. A car is waiting to take you back to your hotel. Please give my deep respects to Dikko and tell him he owes me one thousand yen for repairs to electronic equipment that is the property of the State.'

James Bond took the hard dry paw. He said from his heart:
'Thank you, Mr Tanaka.' He walked out of the little secret room with one thought uppermost in his mind. How fast were Dikko's communications to Melbourne? How fast from Melbourne to London?

6

TIGER, TIGER!

AND now it was a month later and Mr Tanaka had become 'Tiger' and Commander Bond had become 'Bondo-san'. Tiger had explained his name for James Bond. 'James,' he had said. 'That is a difficult work in Japanese. And it does not convey sufficient respect. Bond-san is too much like the Japanese word *bonsan*, which means a priest, a greybeard. The hard consonants at the end of "Bond" are also not easy for the Japanese, and when these occur in a foreign word we add an O. So you are Bondo-san. That is acceptable?'

'Does Bondo mean a pig or anything like that in Japanese?'
'No. It has no meaning.'
'Forgive my asking. The Japanese seem to enjoy many private jokes at the expense of the *gaijin*. I referred the other day to a friend of mine called "Monkey" McCall whom we used to call "Munko". You told me that this was an unmentionable word in your language. So I thought "Bondo" might be equally unmentionable.'
'Have no fear. It is totally respectable.'

The weeks had passed without any significant progress in Bond's mission except in the direction of what seemed to be a genuine friendship between Bond, Tiger and Dikko. Outside working hours the three men became wellnigh inseparable, but Bond sensed that on their excursions into the countryside and during their roistering in the evenings he was being constantly, but with great discretion, sized up. Dikko had confirmed Bond's impression. 'I think you're making progress, champ. Tiger would regard it as dishonourable to lead you up the garden path and then pull the rug out from under you with a flat refusal. Something's definitely cooking in the background, but what it is I haven't the faintest idea. I guess the ball's with Tiger's superiors, but with Tiger on your side. And, in the vernacular, Tiger's got what's called "a broad face". That means he has great powers as a fixer. And this ON he's got in respect of Britain is a huge factor in your favour. What he gave you on your first meeting was an unheard-of *presento*, as we call it here. But watch out! You're piling up a great heap of ON in respect of Tiger. And if it comes to striking a bargain, I hope you've got a pretty massive *presento* up your sleeve so that the ON on both sides is more or less evenly balanced. None of this salmon and shrimp business! Have got? Can do?'

'I'm not so sure,' said Bond doubtfully. The Macao 'Blue Route' material had already dwindled in his mind to the size of a minnow in comparison with the salmon that was Tiger's to give or withhold. The impact of the single slice he had handed Bond had already been formidable. The test of the 200-megaton bomb had duly taken place and had been greeted by the public uproar anticipated by Moscow. But counter-action by the West had been swift. On the excuse of protecting Soviet personnel in England from demonstrations of public animosity, they had been confined within a radius of twenty miles of their homes, and 'for their protection' police were thick round the Soviet Embassy, the consulates and their various trading offices. There had, of course, been reprisals on British diplomats and journalists in Russia, but these were to have been expected. Then President Kennedy had come out with the strongest speech of his career, and had committed total reprisals from the United States in the event of a single nuclear device being exploded by the Soviet Union in any country in the world outside Soviet territory. This thundering pronouncement, which had produced a growl of dismay from the American man-in-the-street, was greeted from Moscow by the feeble riposte that they would take similar action in answer to any Western nuclear device exploded on the territory of the USSR or her allies.

A few days later Bond had been summoned again to Tiger's underground hideout. 'You will not of course repeat this,' Tiger had said with his wicked smile. 'But action in respect of the matter of which you are privately aware has been indefinitely postponed by the Central Authority.'

'Thank you for this private information,' Bond had said. 'But you do realize how your kindness of three weeks ago has greatly alleviated the international tension, particularly in relation to my country. My country would be immensely grateful if they knew of your personal generosity to me. Have I grounds for hoping for your further indulgence?' Bond had got used to the formalities of Oriental circumlocution, although he had not yet attained the refinements of Dikko's speech with Tiger, which included at least one four-letter word in each flowery sentence and which caused Tiger much amusement.

'Bondo-san, this implement which you wish to rent from us, in the most improbable event that it is made available, will command a very high price. As a fair trader, what has your country to offer in exchange for the full use of MAGIC 44?'

'We have a most important intelligence network in China known as the Macao "Blue Route". The fruits of this source would be placed entirely at your disposal.'

Melancholy settled over Tiger's massive face, but deep down in the Tartar eyes there was a wicked gleam. 'I am very much afraid that I have bad news for you, Bondo-san. "Blue Route" has been penetrated by my organization almost since its inception. We already receive the entire fruits of that source. I could show you the files if you wish. We have simply renamed it "Route Orange", and I admit that the material is very acceptable. But we already have it. What other goods had you in mind for exchange?'

Bond had to laugh. The pride of Section J – and of M., for that matter! The work, the expense, the danger of running the 'Blue Route'. And at least fifty per cent in aid of Japan! By God, his eyes were being opened on this trip. This news would put a fine cat among the pigeons at HQ. He said blandly, 'We have many other commodities. Now that you have demonstrated the undoubted value of your implement, may I suggest that you name your price?'

'You believe that you have something on your shelves that is of comparable value? Perhaps material from a similar, though no doubt inferior, source that would be of equal importance in the defence of *our* country?'

'Undoubtedly,' said Bond staunchly. 'But, my dear Tiger, would it not be a good idea, once your mind is made up, for you to pay a visit to London and inspect the shelves for yourself? I am sure my Chief would be honoured to receive you.'

'You do not possess full powers of negotiation?'

'That would be impossible, my dear Tiger. Our security is such that even I have not full knowledge of all our merchandise. So far as I personally am concerned, I am only in a position to pass on to my Chief the substance of what you say or to render you any other personal services you might ask of me.'

For a moment, Tiger Tanaka looked thoughtful. He seemed to be turning Bond's last words over in his mind. Then he closed the interview with the invitation to the geisha restaurant, and Bond went off with mixed feelings to report to Melbourne and London what he had gleaned.

In the room where he now sat after the geisha party, and where Tiger had just cheerfully threatened him with death, tigers' heads snarled at him from the walls and gnashed at him from the floor. His ashtray was enclosed in a stuffed tiger's paw and the chair in which he was sitting was upholstered in tiger's skin. Mr Tanaka had been born in the year of the Tiger, whereas Bond, as Tiger had taken much pleasure in telling him, had been born in the year of the Rat.

Bond took a deep drink of *sake* and said, 'My dear Tiger, I would hate to put you to the inconvenience of having to remove me from the face of the earth. You mean that this time the cedar may not bow before the typhoon? So be it. This time you have my very topmost word of honour.'

Tiger pulled up a chair and faced Bond across the low drink table. He poured himself a liberal tot of Suntory and splashed in the soda. The sound of night traffic from the main Tokyo–Yokohama road came in from some way beyond the surrounding houses, only a few of which now showed doll's-house squares of yellow light. It was the end of September, but warm. It was ten minutes to midnight. Tiger began talking in a soft voice. 'In that case, my dear Bondo-san, and since I know you to be a man of honour, except, of course, in matters affecting your country, which this does not, I will tell you quite an interesting story. This is how it is.' He got out of his chair and sat down on the *tatami* and arranged himself in the lotus position. He was obviously more comfortable in this posture. He said, in an expository tone of voice, 'Ever since the beginning of the era of Meiji, who you will know was the Emperor who fathered the modernization and Westernization of Japan from the beginning of his reign nearly a hundred years ago, there have from time to time been foreigners who have come to this country and settled here. They have for the most part been cranks and scholars, and the European-born American Lafcadio Hearn, who became a Japanese citizen, is a very typical example. In general, they have been tolerated, usually with some amusement. So, perhaps, would be a Japanese who bought a castle in the Highlands of Scotland, and who learned and spoke Gaelic with his neighbours and expressed unusual and often impertinent interest in Scottish folkways. If he went about his researches politely and peaceably, he would be dubbed an amiable eccentric. And so it has been with the Westerners who have settled and spent their lives in Japan, though occasionally, in time of war, as would no doubt be the case with our mythical Japanese in Scotland, they have been regarded as spies and suffered internment and hardship. Now, since the occupation, there have been many such settlers, the great majority of whom, as you can imagine, have been American. The Oriental way of life is particularly attractive to the American who wishes to escape from a culture which, I am sure you will agree, has become, to say the least of it, more and more unattractive except to the lower grades of the human species to whom bad but plentiful food, shiny toys such as the automobile and the television, and the "quick buck", often dishonestly earned, or earned in exchange for minimal labour or skills, are the *summum bonum*, if you will allow the sentimental echo from my Oxford education.'

'I will,' said Bond. 'But is this not a picture of the life that is being officially encouraged in your own country?'

Tiger Tanaka's face darkened perceptibly. 'For the time being,' he said with distaste, 'we are being subjected to what I can best describe as the "Scuola di Coca-Cola". Baseball, amusement arcades, hot dogs, hideously large bosoms, neon lighting – these are the part of our payment for defeat in battle. They are the tepid tea of the way of life we know under the name of *demokorasu*. They are a frenzied denial of the official scapegoats for our defeat – a denial of the spirit of the *samurai* as expressed in the *kami-kaze*, a denial of our ancestors, a denial of our gods. They are a despicable way of life' – Tiger almost spat the words – 'but fortunately they are also expendable and temporary. They have as much importance in the history of Japan as the life of a dragonfly.' He paused. 'But to return to my story. Our American residents are of a sympathetic type – on a low level of course. They enjoy the subservience, which I may say is only superficial, of our women. They enjoy the remaining strict patterns of our life – the symmetry, compared with the chaos that reigns in America. They enjoy our simplicity, with its underlying hint of deep meaning, as expressed for instance in the tea ceremony, flower arrangements, NO plays – none of which of course they understand. They also enjoy, because they have no ancestors and probably no family life worth speaking of, our veneration of the old and our worship of the past. For, in their impermanent world, they recognize these as permanent things just as, in their ignorant and childish way, they admire the fictions of the Wild West and other American myths that have become known to them, not through their education, of which they have none, but through television.'

'This is tough stuff, Tiger. I've got a lot of American friends who don't equate with what you're saying. Presumably you're talking of the lower level G Is – second-generation Americans who are basically Irish or Germans or Czechs or Poles who probably ought to be working in the fields or coalmines of their countries of origin instead of swaggering around a conquered country under the blessed coverlet of the Stars and Stripes with too much money to spend. I daresay they occasionally marry a Japanese girl and settle down here. But surely they pull up stumps pretty quickly. Our Tommies have done the same thing in Germany. But that's quite a different thing from the Lafcadio Hearns of the world.'

Tiger Tanaka bowed almost to the ground. 'Forgive me, Bondo-san. Of course you are right, and I have been diverted from my story down most unworthy paths. I did not ask you here to pour out my innermost repugnance at the occupation of my country. This of course is repugnance against the fact of defeat. I apologize. And of course you are correct. There are many cultured Americans who have taken up residence in this country and who are most valued citizens. You are right to correct me, for I have friends of this nature, in the arts, the sciences, in literature, and they are indeed valued members of the community. I was, let us say, letting off steam. You understand?'

'Of course, Tiger. My country has not been occupied for many centuries. The imposition of a new culture on an old one is something we have not suffered. I cannot imagine my reactions in the same circumstances. Much the same as yours, I expect. Please go on with your story.' Bond reached for the *sake* flask. It stood in a jar of warm water being heated over a slow flame from a charcoal burner. He filled his glass and drank. Tiger Tanaka rocked two or three times on his buttocks and the sides of his feet. He resumed.

'As I have said, there are a number of foreigners who have taken up residence in Japan and, for the most part, they are inoffensive eccentrics. But there is one such person who entered the country in January of this year who has revealed himself to be an eccentric of the most devilish nature. This man is a monster. You may laugh, Bondo-san, but this man is no less than a fiend in human form.'

'I have met many bad men in my time, Tiger, and generally they have been slightly mad. Is that the case in this instance?'

'Very much the reverse. The calculated ingenuity of this man, his understanding of the psychology of my people, show him to be a man of quite outstanding genius. In the opinion of our highest scholars and savants he is a scientific research worker and collector probably unique in the history of the world.'

'What does he collect?'

'He collects death.'

7

THE DEATH COLLECTOR

JAMES BOND smiled at this dramatic utterance. 'A collector of death? You mean he kills people?'

'No, Bondo-san. It is not as simple as that. He persuades, or rather entices people to kill themselves.' Tiger paused, the wide expanse of his brow furrowed. 'No, that also is not being just. Let us just say that he provides an easy and attractive opportunity – a resort – for people to do away with themselves. His present tally, in just under six months, is something over five hundred Japanese.'

'Why don't you arrest him, hang him?'

'Bondo-san, it is not as easy as that. I had better begin at the beginning. In January of this year, there entered the country, quite legally, a gentleman by the name of Doctor Guntram Shatterhand. He was accompanied by Frau Emmy Shatterhand, born de Bedon. They had Swiss passports and the doctor described himself as a horticulturalist and botanist specializing in sub-tropical species. He carried high references from the Jardin des Plantes in Paris, Kew Gardens, and other authorities, but these were couched in rather nebulous terms. He quickly got in touch with the equivalent authorities in Japan and with experts in the Ministry of Agriculture, and these gentlemen were astonished and delighted to learn that Doctor Shatterhand was prepared to spend no less than one million pounds on establishing an exotic garden or park in this country which he would stock with a priceless collection of rare plants and shrubs from all over the world. These he would import at his own expense in a sufficient state of maturity to allow his park to be planted with the minimum of delay – an extremely expensive procedure if you know anything about horticulture.'

'I know nothing about it. Like the Texan millionaires who import fully-grown palms and tropical shrubs from Florida?'

'Exactly. Well, the park was not to be open to the public, but would be freely available for study and research work by authorized Japanese experts. All right. A wonderful offer that was enthusiastically accepted by the government, who, in return, granted the good doctor a ten-year residence permit – a very rare privilege. Meanwhile, as a matter of routine, the Immigration authorities made inquiries about the doctor through my department. Since I have no representative in Switzerland, I referred the matter to our friends of the CIA, and in due course he was given complete clearance. It appeared that he was of Swedish origin and was not widely known in Switzerland, where he only possessed the minimum requirement for residential status in the shape of two rooms in an apartment block in Lausanne. But his financial standing with the Union de Banques Suisses was Grade One, which I understand requires you to be a millionaire many times over. Since money is almost the unique status symbol in Switzerland, his clearance by the Swiss was impeccable, though no information could be obtained about his standing as a botanist. Kew and the Jardin des Plantes, on inquiry, referred to him as an enthusiastic amateur who had made valuable contributions to these institutions in the form of tropical and sub-tropical species collected for him by expeditions which he had financed. So! An interesting and financially sound citizen whose harmless pursuits would be of some benefit to Japan. Yes?'

'Sounds like it.'

'After travelling round the country in great style, the doctor took a fancy to a semi-ruined castle in Kyūshū, our southern island. The castle was in an extremely remote corner of the coast not far from Fukuoka, the principal prefecture of the island, and in ancient times it had been one of a line of castles facing the Tsushima Straits, the scene of the famous defeat of the Russian navy. These castles were originally designed to repel attacks from the Korean mainland. Most of them had fallen into disrepair, but the one chosen by the doctor was a giant edifice that had been occupied until the last war by a rich and eccentric family of textile millionaires, and its monumental surrounding wall was just what the doctor required for the privacy of his undertaking. An army of builders and decorators moved in. Meanwhile, the plants ordered by the doctor began arriving from all over the world and, with a blanket customs clearance from the Ministry of Agriculture, they were planted in appropriate soils and settings. Here I should mention that an additional reason for the doctor's choice of site was that the property, which extends for some five hundred acres, is highly volcanic and furnished with many geysers and fumaroles, which are common in Japan. These would provide, all the year round, the temperature needed for the successful propagation of these tropical shrubs, trees and plants from the equatorial zones. The doctor and his wife, who is by the way extremely ugly, moved into the castle with all speed and set about recruiting staff in the neighbourhood who would look after the establishment and its grounds.' Here Tiger assumed his sorrowful face. 'And it was at this time that I should not have dismissed as fanciful certain reports that reached me from the Chief of Police at Fukuoka. These were to the effect that the doctor was recruiting his staff uniquely from former members of the Black Dragon Society.'

'And what might that be?'

'Have been,' Tiger corrected him. 'The Society was officially disbanded before the war. But in its heyday it was the most feared and powerful secret society in Japan. It consisted originally of the dregs of the *sōshi* – the unemployed *samurai* who were left high and dry after the Meiji Restoration of about a hundred years ago – but it later recruited terrorists, gangsters, Fascist politicos, cashiered officers from the navy and army, secret agents, soldiers of fortune and other riff-raff, but also big men in industry and finance, and even the occasional Cabinet Minister who found Black Dragon support of much practical value when dirty work had to be done. And the odd thing is, though it does not seem so odd to me today, that the doctor should have chosen his site, leaving out its practical amenities, in just that corner of Japan that used to be the headquarters of the Black Dragons and has always been a hotbed of extremists. Toyama Mitsuru, the former head of the Black Dragons, came from Fukuoka; so did the anarchist Hirota, and Nakano, leader of the former Tohokai, or Fascist group, in the Diet. It has always been a nest of scoundrels, this district, and it remains so today. These extreme sects never die out completely, as you have recently, my dear Bondo-san, found in the resurgence of the Black Shirts in England, and this Doctor Shatterhand found no difficulty in collecting some twenty extremely tough and dangerous characters around him, all most correctly clothed as servants and gardeners and, no doubt, perfectly good at their ostensible jobs. On one occasion the Prefect of Police thought it his duty to make a courtesy call and give his distinguished inhabitant a word of caution. But the doctor dismissed the matter on the grounds that competent guards would be necessary to maintain his privacy and keep trespassers away from his valuable collection of plants. This seemed reasonable enough, and anyway the doctor appeared to be under high patronage in Tokyo. The Prefect bowed himself out, much impressed with the lavish display of wealth in evidence in the heart of his poor province.'

Tiger Tanaka paused and poured more *sake* for Bond and

more Suntory for himself. Bond took the opportunity to ask just how dangerous this Black Dragon Society had really been. Was it the equivalent of the Chinese *tongs*?

'Much more powerful. You have heard of the Ching-Pang and Hung-Pang *tongs* that were so much feared in China in the days of the Kuomintang. No? Well the Black Dragons were a hundred times worse. To have them on your heels was certain death. They were totally ruthless, and not out of any particular political conviction. They operated strictly for cash.'

'Well, under this doctor from Switzerland, have they done any harm yet?'

'Oh no. They are nothing more than he says – personal staff, at the worst, if you like, a bodyguard. No. The trouble is quite different, much more complex. You see, this man Shatterhand has created what I can only describe as a garden of death.'

Bond raised his eyebrows. Really, for the head of a national secret service, Tiger's metaphors were almost ridiculously dramatic.

Tiger exploded his golden smile. 'Bondo-san, I can see from your face that you think I am either drunk or mad. Now listen. This Doctor Shatterhand has filled this famous park of his uniquely with poisonous vegetation, the lakes and streams with poisonous fish, and he has infested the place with snakes, scorpions and poisonous spiders. He and this hideous wife of his are not harmed by these things, because whenever they leave the castle he wears full suits of armour of the seventeenth century, and she wears some other kind of protective clothing. His workers are not harmed because they wear rubber boots up to the knee, and *maskos*, that is, antiseptic gauze masks such as many people in Japan wear over the mouth and nose to avoid infection or the spreading of infection.'

'What a daft set-up.'

Tiger reached into the folds of the *yukata* he had changed into when they entered the house. He brought out several sheets of paper pinned together. He handed them over to Bond and said, 'Be patient. Do not judge what you do not understand. I know nothing of these poisonous plants. Nor, I expect, do you. Here is a list of those that have so far been planted by this doctor, together with comments by our Ministry of Agriculture. Read it. Take your time. You will be interested to learn what charming vegetation grows on the surface of the globe.'

Bond took the papers. The first page was a general note on vegetable poisons. There followed an annotated list. The papers bore the seal of the Ministry of Agriculture. This is what he read:

The poisons listed fall into six main categories:

1. *Deliriant.* Symptoms: spectral illusions, delirium; dilated pupils; thirst and dryness; incoordination; then paralysis and spasms.

2. *Inebriant.* Symptoms: excitement of cerebral functions and of circulation; loss of coordination and muscular movements; double vision; then sleep and deep coma.

3. *Convulsivant.* Symptoms: intermittent spasms, from head downwards. Death from exhaustion, usually within three hours, or rapid recovery.

4. *Depressant.* Symptoms: vertigo, vomiting, abdominal pain, confused vision, convulsions, paralysis, fainting, sometimes asphyxia.

5. *Asthenic.* Symptoms: numbness, tingling mouth, abdominal pain, vertigo, vomiting, purging, delirium, paralysis, fainting.

6. *Irritant.* Symptoms: burning pain in throat and stomach, thirst, nausea, vomiting. Death by shock, convulsions or exhaustion; or starvation by injury to throat or stomach.

SPECIMENS LISTED BY CUSTOMS AND EXCISE
DEPARTMENT AS IMPORTED BY DOCTOR GUNTRAM
SHATTERHAND

Jamaica dogwood, fish-poison tree (Piscidia erythrina): Tree, 30 ft. White and blood-coloured flowers. Inebriant. Toxic principle: piscidine. W. Indies.

Nux-vomica tree, poison-nut, crow-fig, kachita (Strychnos nux-

vomica): Tree 40 ft. Smooth bark, attractive fruits, which have bitter taste. Greenish-white flowers. Seeds most poisonous part. Convulsivant. Toxic principle: strychnine, brucine. S. India, Java.

Guiana poison-tree (Strychnos toxifera): curare arrow-poison taken from bark. Creeper. Death within one hour from respiratory paralysis. Toxic principles: curare, strychnine, brucine. Guiana.

St Ignatius's bean (Strychnos Ignatii): small tree, seeds yield brucine. Convulsivant. Philippines.

False Upas-tree (Strychnos tieuté): large climbing shrub. Strychnine or brucine from leaf, seed, stem or root-bark. Java.

East Indian snakewood (Strychnos colubrina): climbing tree. Yields strychnine, brucine. Convulsivant. Java, Timor.

Ipecacuanha (Psychotria ipecacuanha): shrubby plant. Depressant. Toxic principle: emetine, from root. Brazil.

White-woolly Kombe bean, Gaboon arrow poison (Stropanthus hispidus): woody climber, 6 ft. Toxic principle: strophanthin, incine. Asthenic. W. Africa.

Ordeal-tree, poison tanghin (Tanghinia venenifera or cerbera tanghin): small evergreen tree, 20 ft. Fruit purplish, tinged with green. Toxic principle: tanghinine, cerberin. Asthenic. Madagascar.

Upas-tree, Malay arrow-poison tree (Antiaria toxicaria): jungle tree – 100 ft. before branches start. Wood light, white, hard, milk-bearing. Toxic principle: antiarin, from milky sap. Asthenic. Java, Borneo, Sumatra, Philippines.

Poison ivy, trailing poison oak (Rhus toxicodendron): climbing shrub. Greenish-yellow flowers. Stem contains milky juice – irritant. Toxic principle: toxicodendrol. USA.

Yellow oleander, campanilla, be-still tree (Thevetia peruviana): small tree. All parts can be fatally toxic, particularly fruit. Pulse slows, vomiting, shock. Hawaii.

Castor bean plant (Ricinus communis): seeds are source of castor oil, also contain toxic principle, ricin. Harmless if eaten. If it enters the circulation through scratch or abrasion is fatal within 7–10 days. One hundredth of a milligram can kill a 200 lb. man. Loss of appetite, emesis, purgation, delirium, collapse and death. Hawaii, S. America.

Common oleander (Nerium Indicum): evergreen shrub. The roots, bark, juice, flowers and leaves all fatally toxic. Acts chiefly on the heart. Used in India as leprosy treatment, abortifacient, means of suicide. India, Hawaii. One death was due to the victim's having eaten meat cooked over an open fire, spitted on a stick of oleander wood.

Rosary pea, crab's eye, Jequiritz bean (Abrus precatorius): climbing shrub. Small shiny red seeds weight average 1.75 grains, used by Indian goldsmiths as weights. Seeds are ground down into a paste with a little cold water, made into small pointed cylinders. If these are inserted beneath skin of human or animal death occurs within four hours. India, Hawaii.

Jimson weed (Datura stramonium): variety of thorn apple plant, found in N. Africa, India. Also: *Ololiuqui (D. mete-loides)* from Mexico, and *D. tatula* from Central and South America. All three are hallucinatory. *D. stramonium's* apples are smoked by Arabs and Swahilis, leaves eaten by E. African Negroes, seeds added to hashish and leaves to hemp by Bengalese Indians. *D. tatula* was used as a truth-drug by Zapotec Indians in courts of law. Addiction to toloachi, a drink made from *D. tatula*, causes chronic imbecility.

Gloriosa superba: spectacularly beautiful climbing lily. Roots, stalks, leaves contain an acrid narcotic, superbine, as well as colchicine and choline. Three grains of colchicine are fatal. Hawaii.

Sand-box tree (Hura crepitans): whole tree contains an active emetocathartic, used as a fish-poison in Brazil. Also contains crepitin, same group of poisons as ricin. Harmless if swallowed, must be taken into circulation through wound to be fatal. Death comes in 7–10 days. C. and S. America.

Pride-of-India, Chinaberry tree, China tree (Melia azedarach): small tree. Beautiful dark-green leaves, lavender blossoms. Fruit contains toxic narcotic which attacks entire central nervous system. Hawaii, C. and S. America.

Physic nut (*Jatropha curcas*): bushy tree. Raw seeds violently purgative, often fatal due to exhaustion. Caribbean.

Mexican tuber, camotillo: wild potato, grows generally. According to Indian tradition, it is plucked during the waning of the moon; it is alleged to begin deadly action the same number of days after consumption as it was stored after being dug up. Toxic principle: solanine. Central and S. America.

Divine mushroom (*Amanita mexicana*): closely related to European Fly Agaric. Black mushroom, eaten fresh or steeped in warm milk laced with agave spirits. Causes hypersensitivity of the skin surface, ultra-acute hearing and sight, then hallucinations of several hours, followed by deep melancholia. Active principle unknown. Central and S. America.

Bond finished his reading. He handed the papers back. He said, 'Doctor Shatterhand's garden is indeed a lovesome thing, God wot.'

'And you have of course heard of the South American piranha fish? They can strip a whole horse to the bones in less than an hour. The scientific name is Serrasalmus. The subspecies Nattereri is the most voracious. Our good doctor has preferred these fish to our native goldfish for his lakes. You see what I mean?'

'No,' said Bond, 'frankly I don't. What's the object of the good doctor's exercise?'

8

SLAY IT WITH FLOWERS

IT WAS three o'clock in the morning. The noise of the traffic to Yokohama had died. James Bond didn't feel tired. He was now totally absorbed in this extraordinary story of the Swiss doctor, who, as Tiger had originally said, 'collected death'.

Tiger wasn't telling him this bizarre case history for his entertainment. There was going to come a moment of climax. What would that climax be?

Tiger wiped his hand over his face. He said, 'Did you read a story in the evening edition of the *Asahi* today? It concerned a suicide.'

'No.'

'This was a young student aged eighteen who had failed his examination for the university for the second time. He lived in the suburbs of Tokyo. There was construction work on a new *departmento*, a department store, going on near where he lived. He went out of his room on to the site. A pile-driver was at work, sinking the foundations. Suddenly this youth broke through the surrounding workmen and, as the pile came crashing down, laid his head on the block beneath it.'

'What a ghastly business! Why?'

'He had brought dishonour on his parents, his ancestors. This was his way of expiation. Suicide is a most unfortunate aspect of the Japanese way of life.' Tiger paused. 'Or perhaps a most noble one. It depends how you look at it. That boy, and his family, will have gained great face in his neighbourhood.'

'You can't gain face from strawberry jam.'

'Think again, Bondo-san. Your posthumous VCs, for instance?'

'They're not awarded for committing suicide after failing in an examination.'

'We are not so *demokorasu* as you are.' There was irony in Tiger's voice. 'Dishonour must be expunged – according to those of us who remain what you would describe as old-fashioned. There is no apology more sincere than the offering up of your own life. It is literally all you have to give.'

'But even if this boy failed for the university, he could have gone for a lower standard of examination, for a lower grade of college. As you know, we say "Blast!" or perhaps a stronger word if we fail an examination in Britain. But we readjust our sights, or our parents do it for us, and have another bash. We don't kill ourselves. It wouldn't occur to us. It would be dishonourable rather than honourable. It would be cowardly – a refusal to stand up to reverses, to life. And it would give great pain to our parents, and certainly no satisfaction to our ancestors.'

'With us it is different. And despite *demokorasu*, the parents of this youth will be rejoicing this evening and their neighbours will be rejoicing with them. Honour is more important to us than life – more proud, more beautiful.'

Bond shrugged. 'Well, I just think that if the boy had the guts to do this thing, it was the waste of a perfectly good Japanese life. In fact, of course, this suicide business in Japan is nothing more than a form of hysteria – an expression of the streak of violence that seems to run all through the history of Japan. If you hold your own life so cheaply, it follows that you will hold others' lives even more cheaply. The other day, I saw a traffic accident at one of the main crossings. I don't know the name of it. It was a multiple affair, and there were bodies all over the place. The police came, but instead of concentrating on getting the wounded to hospital, insisted that they should lie where they were so that they could draw chalk lines round them and photograph them – presumably for use when the case came to court.'

'That is common practice,' said Tiger indifferently. 'We are much over-populated. Abortion is legal. It is helping to solve one of our problems if a few extra people die in an automobile accident. But there is something in what you said earlier. Our word for suicide is *jisatsu*, literally "self-murder", and although it is a violent solution to a personal problem, it carries no stigma as it would in your country. In fact, one of our most famous folk-tales, known to all children, is of the forty-seven *ronin*, or bodyguards. Through their negligence, their lord, Asano, was assassinated. They swore to avenge him and they did so. But then they came together at a place called Ako and all committed *seppuku* to expiate their negligence. This is what you know as *hara-kiri*, which is a vulgar term meaning "belly-cutting". Today, at the time of the festival at the Ako shrine, special trains have to be laid on to accommodate the respectful pilgrims.'

'Well, if you bring your children up on that sort of stuff, you can't expect them not to venerate the act of suicide.'

'Just so,' said Tiger proudly, '25,000 Japanese commit suicide every year. Only the bureaucrats regard that as a shameful statistic. And the more spectacular the suicide, the more warmly it is approved. Not long ago, a young student achieved great renown by trying to saw his own head off. Lovers link hands and throw themselves over the very high Kegon Falls at Nikko. The Mihara volcano on the island of Oshima is another favourite locale. People run down the roasting slope of the crater and hurl themselves, their shoes on fire, into the bubbling cauldron in its centre. To combat this popular pastime, the interfering authorities have now opened, at great expense, a "Suicide Prevention Office" on the peak. But always the wheels of the good old-fashioned railway train provide the most convenient guillotine. They have the merit of being self-operating. All you need to do is make a four-foot jump.'

'You're a bloodthirsty old bastard, Tiger. But what's all this lecture about anyway? What's it got to do with friend Shatterhand and his pretty garden?'

'Everything, Bondo-san. Everything. You see, much against the good doctor's wishes of course, his poison garden has become the most desirable site for suicides in the whole of Japan. It has everything – a ride on our famous "Romance" express to Kyoto; a boat trip across our beautiful Inland Sea that is so full of Japanese history; a local train from the terminal harbour at Beppu to Fukuoka and a walk or taxi drive along a beautiful coast to the awe-inspiring ramparts of this mysterious Castle of Death. Climb these, or smuggle yourself in on a provision cart, and then a last delicious, ruminative walk, perhaps hand-in-hand with your lover, through the beautiful groves. And finally the great gamble, the game of *pachinko* the Japanese love so much. Which ball will have your number on it? Will your death be easy or painful? Will a Russell's Viper strike at your legs as you walk the silent, well-raked paths? Will some kindly, deadly dew fall upon you during the night as you rest under this or that gorgeous tree? Or will hunger or curiosity lead you to munch a handful of those red berries or pick one of those orange fruit? Of course, if you want to make it quick, there is always a bubbling, sulphurous fumarole at hand. In any one of those, the thousand degrees Centigrade will allow you just enough time for one scream. The place is nothing more than a *departmento* of death, its shelves laden with delicious packages of self-destruction, all given away for nothing. Can you not imagine that old and young flock there as if to a shrine? The police have erected a barricade across the road. Genuine visitors, botanists and so on, have to show a pass. But the suicides fight their way to the shrine across the fields and marshes, scrabble at the great walls, break their nails to gain entrance. The good doctor is of course much dismayed. He has erected stern notices of warning, with skulls and crossbones upon them. They act only as advertisements! He has even gone to the expense of flying one of those high helium balloons from the roof of his castle. The hanging streamers threaten trespassers with prosecution. But, alas for the doctor's precautions, the high balloon serves only to beckon. Here is death! it proclaims. Come and get it!'

'You're daft, Tiger. Why don't you arrest him? Burn the place down?'

'Arrest him for what? For presenting Japan with this unique collection of rare plants? Burn down a million-pound establishment belonging to a respected *gaijin* resident? The man has done nothing wrong. If anyone is to blame, it is the Japanese people. It is true that he could exercise more careful surveillance, have his grounds more regularly patrolled. And it is certainly odd that when he has the ambulance called, the victims are always totally dead and are usually in the form of a bag of calcined bones fished out of one of the fumaroles. From the list I have shown you, one would have expected some to be only crippled, or blinded. The Herr Doktor expresses himself as much puzzled. He suggests that, in the cases of blindness or amnesia, the victims presumably fall into one of the fumaroles by mistake. Maybe. But, as I have said, his tally so far is over five hundred and, with the stream of publicity, more and more people will be attracted to the Castle of Death. We have got to put a stop to it.'

'What steps have been taken so far?'

'Commissions of investigation have visited the doctor. They have been most courteously treated. The doctor has begged that something shall be done to protect him from these trespassers. He complains that they interfere with his work, break off precious boughs and pick valuable plants. He shows himself as entirely cooperative with any measures that can be suggested short of abandoning this project, which is so dear to his heart and so much appreciated by the Japanese specialists in botany and so forth. He has made a further most generous offer. He is constructing a research department – to be manned by workers of his own choice, mark you – to extract the poisons from his shrubs and plants and give the essences free to an appropriate medical research centre. You will have noted that many of these poisons are valuable medicines in a diluted form.'

'But how has all this come on your plate?' Bond was now getting drowsy. It was four o'clock and the horizon of jagged grey, porcelain-shingled roof-tops was lightening. He poured down the last of the *sake*. It had the flat taste of too much. It was time he was in bed. But Tiger was obviously obsessed with this lunatic business, and subtle, authentic glimpses of Japan were coming through the ridiculous, nightmare story with its undertones of Poe, Le Fanu, Bram Stoker, Ambrose Bierce.

Tiger seemed unaffected by the lateness of the hour. The *samurai* face was perhaps etched in more sinister, more brutal lines. The hint of Tartar, tamed and civilized, lurked with less concealment, like a caged animal, in the dark pools of his eyes. But the occasional rocking motion on the buttocks and sides of the feet was the only sign that he was interested, even excited. He said, 'One month ago, Bondo-san, I sent one of my best men into this place to try and discover what it was all about. I was so instructed by my Minister, the Minister of the Interior. He in turn was under orders from the Prime Minister. The matter was becoming one of public debate. I chose a good man. He was instructed to get into the place, observe, and report. One week later, Bondo-san, he was recovered from the sea on a beach near this Castle of Death. He was blinded and in delirium. All the lower half of his body was terribly burned. He could only babble a *haiku* about dragonflies. I later discovered that, as a youth, he had indulged in the pastime of our youngsters. He had tied a female dragonfly on a thread and let it go. This acts as a lure for the male dragonfly and you can quickly catch many males in this way. They attach themselves to the female and will not let go. The *haiku* – that is a verse of seventeen syllables – he kept on reciting until his death, which came soon, was "Desolation! Pink dragonflies flitting above the graves." '

James Bond felt he was living inside a dream: the little room, partitioned in imitation rice-paper and cedar ply-wood, the open vista of a small, inscrutable garden in which water tinkled, the distant redness of an imminent dawn, the long background of *sake* and cigarettes, the quiet voice of the storyteller telling a fairy tale, as it might be told in a tent under the stars. And yet this was something that had happened the other day, close by – was happening now, something that Tiger had brought him here to tell. Why? Because he was lonely? Because there was no one else he could trust? Bond pulled himself out of his somnolent slouch. He said, 'I'm sorry, Tiger. What did you do next?'

Tiger Tanaka seemed to sit slightly more upright on his black-edged rectangle of golden *tatami*. He looked very directly at James Bond and said, 'What was there to do? I did nothing except apologize to my superiors. I waited for an honourable solution to present itself. I waited for you to come.'

'Me!'

'You were sent. It might have been another.'

James Bond yawned. He couldn't help it. He could see no end to the evening. Tiger had got some Japanese bee in his Japanese bonnet. How in hell could Bond stop it buzzing? He said, 'Tiger. It's time for bed. Let's talk about the rest of this tomorrow. Of course I'll give you any advice I can. I can see it's a difficult problem. But those are just the ones to sleep on.' He made to rise from his chair.

Tiger said, and it was an order, 'Sit down, Bondo-san. If you have any regard for your country, you leave tomorrow.' He consulted his watch. 'By the twelve-twenty from Tokyo main station. Your ultimate destination is Fukuoka on the southern island of Kyūshū. You will not be going back to your hotel. You will not be seeing Dikko. From now on you are under my personal orders.' The voice went very quiet and velvety. 'Is that understood?'

Bond sat up as if he had been stung. 'What in God's name are you talking about, Tiger?'

Tiger Tanaka said, 'In my office the other day you made a significant statement. You said words to the effect that in exchange for MAGIC 44 you were empowered to carry out any personal services that I might require of you.'

'I didn't say that I was empowered. I meant that I would do anything for you on my personal responsibility.'

'That is quite good enough. I took you at your word and I requested an audience of the Prime Minister. He instructed me to proceed, but to regard the matter as a State secret known only to him and to me – and of course to you.'

'Come on, Tiger,' said Bond impatiently. 'Cut the cackle. What is it you want me to do?'

But Tiger was not to be hurried. He said, 'Bondo-san, I will now be blunt with you, and you will not be offended, because we are friends. Yes? Now it is a sad fact that I, and many of us in positions of authority in Japan, have formed an unsatisfactory opinion about the British people since the war. You have not only lost a great Empire, you have seemed almost anxious to throw it away with both hands. All right,' he held up a hand, 'we will not go deeply into the reasons for this policy, but when you apparently sought to arrest this slide into impotence at Suez, you succeeded only in stage-managing one of the most pitiful bungles in the history of the world, if not the worst. Further, your governments have shown themselves successively incapable of ruling and have handed over effective control of the country to the trade unions, who appear to be dedicated to the principle of doing less and less work for more money. This feather-bedding, this shirking of an honest day's work, is sapping at ever-increasing speed the moral fibre of the British, a quality the world once so much admired. In its place we now see a vacuous, aimless horde of seekers-after-pleasure – gambling at the pools and bingo, whining at the weather and the declining fortunes of the country, and wallowing nostalgically in gossip about the doings of the Royal Family and of your so-called aristocracy in the pages of the most debased newspapers in the world.'

James Bond roared with laughter. 'You've got a bloody cheek, Tiger! You ought to write that out and sign it "Octo-genarian" and send it in to *The Times*. You just come over and take a look at the place. It's not doing all that badly.'

'Bondo-san, you have pleaded guilty out of your own mouth. "Not doing too badly," indeed! That is the cry-baby excuse of a boy who gets a thoroughly bad end-of-term report. In fact you are doing very badly indeed in the opinion of your few remaining friends. And now you come to me and ask for some very important intelligence material to bolster up the pitiful ruins of a once great Power. Why should we give it to you? What good will it do us? What good will it do you, Bondo-san? It is like giving smelling salts to a punch-drunk heavy-weight just before the inevitable knock-out.'

Bond said angrily, 'Balls to you, Tiger! And balls again! Just because you're a pack of militant potential murderers here, longing to get rid of your American masters and play at being *samurai* again, snarling behind your subservient smiles, you only judge people by your own jungle standards. Let me tell you this, my fine friend. England may have been bled pretty thin by a couple of World Wars, our Welfare State politics may have made us expect too much for free, and the liberation of our Colonies may have gone too fast, but we still climb Everest and beat plenty of the world at plenty of sports and win Nobel Prizes. Our politicians may be a feather pated bunch, and I expect yours are too. All politicians are. But there's nothing wrong with the British people – although there are only fifty million of them.'

Tiger Tanaka smiled happily. 'Well spoken, Bondo-san. I thought your famous English stoicism might break down if I hit hard enough. I just wanted to see. And, for your information, those are very similar to the words I addressed to my Prime Minister. And do you know what he said? He said, all right, Mr Tanaka. Put this Commander Bond to the test. If he succeeds, I will agree that there is still an *élite* in Britain and that this valuable material would be safe in their hands. If he fails, you will politely turn down the request.'

Bond shrugged impatiently. He was still smarting under Tiger's onslaught, and the half-truths which he knew lay behind his words. 'All right, Tiger. What is this ridiculous test? Some typical bit of *samurai* nonsense, I suppose.'

'More or less,' agreed Tiger Tanaka, with equanimity. 'You are to enter this Castle of Death and slay the Dragon within.'

*

9

INSTANT JAPAN

THE black Topoyet hurtled through the deserted streets which were shiny with the dew of what would be a beautiful day.

Tiger had dressed in casual clothes as if for a country outing. He had a small overnight bag on the seat beside him. They were on the way to a bathhouse which Tiger said was of a very special, a very pleasurable nature. It was also, Tiger said, very discreet, and the opportunity would be taken to make a start in transforming Bond's appearance into something more closely resembling a Japanese.

Tiger had overridden all Bond's objections. On all the evidence, this doctor was a purveyor of death. Because he was mad? Because it amused him? Tiger neither knew nor cared. For obvious reasons of policy, his assassination, which

had been officially agreed to, could not be carried out by a
Japanese. Bond's appearance on the scene was therefore very
timely. He had had much practice in such clandestine oper-
ations and, if he was subsequently arrested by the Japanese
police, an adequate cover story involving foreign intelligence
services could be cooked up. He would be tried, sentenced,
and then quietly smuggled out of the country. If he failed,
then presumably the doctor or his guards would kill him.
That would be too bad. Bond argued that he had personally
nothing against this Swiss botanist. Tiger replied that any
good man's hand would be against a man who had already
killed five hundred of his fellow creatures. Was that not so?
And, in any case, Bond was being hired to do this act in
exchange for MAGIC 44. Did that not quieten his conscience?
Bond agreed reluctantly that it did. As a last resort, Bond
said that the operation was in any case impossible. A foreigner
in Japan could be spotted five miles away. Tiger replied that
this matter had been provided for and the first step was a visit
to this most discreet bathhouse. Here Bond would receive his
first treatment and then get some sleep before catching the
train on which Tiger would be accompanying him. And Tiger,
with a devilish grin, had assured him that at any rate part of
his treatment would be most pleasurable and relaxing.

The exterior of the bathhouse looked like a Japanese inn
– some carefully placed stepping-stones meandering briefly
between dwarf pines, a wide-open, yellow-lighted doorway
with a vista of polished wood floors behind, three bowing
smiling women in traditional dress, as bright as birds although
it was nearly five in the morning, and the inevitable row of
spotless but undersized slippers. After much bowing and
counter-bowing and a few phrases from Tiger, Bond took
off his shoes and, in his socks (explanation by Tiger; polite
giggles behind raised hands), did as Tiger told him and
followed one of the women along a gleaming corridor and
through an open partition that revealed a miniature combination of a bedroom and a Turkish bath. A young girl,
wearing nothing but tight, brief shorts and an exiguous white
brassière, bowed low, said, 'Excuse, please,' and began to

unbutton Bond's trousers. Bond held the pretty hand where it was. He turned to the older woman who was about to close the partition and said, 'Tanaka-san,' in a voice that pleaded and ordered. Tiger was fetched. He was wearing nothing but his underpants. He said, 'What is it now?'

Bond said, 'Now listen, Tiger, I'm sure this pretty girl and I will get along very well indeed. But just tell me what the menu is. Am I going to eat her or is she going to eat me?'

Tiger said patiently, 'You really must learn to obey orders without asking questions, Bondo-san. That is the essence of our relationship during the next few days. You see that box? When she has undressed you, she will put you in the box which has a charcoal fire under it. You will sweat. After perhaps ten minutes she will help you out of the box and wash you from head to foot. She will even tenderly clean out your ears with a special ivory instrument. She will then pour a very tenacious dark dye with which she has been supplied into that tiled bath in the floor and you will get in. You will relax and bathe your face and hair. She will then dry you and cut your hair in the Japanese style. She will then give you a massage on that couch and, according to your indications, she will make this massage as delightful, as prolonged as you wish. You will then go to sleep. When you are awakened with eggs and bacon and coffee you will kiss the girl good morning and shave, or the other way round, and that will be that.' Tiger curtly asked the girl a question. She brushed back her bang of black hair coquettishly and replied. 'The girl says she is eighteen and that her name is Mariko Ichiban. Mariko means "Truth" and Ichiban means "Number One". The girls in these establishments are numbered. And now, please don't disturb me any more. I am about to enjoy myself in a similar fashion, but without the walnut stain. And please, in future, have faith. You are about to undergo a period of entirely new sensations. They may be strange and surprising. They will not be painful – while you are under my authority, that is. Savour them. Enjoy them as if each one was your last. All right? Then good night, my dear Bondo-san. The night will be short, alas, but if you embrace it fully, it

will be totally delightful up to the last squirm of ecstasy. And,'
Tiger gave a malicious wave of the hand as he went out and
closed the partition, 'you will arise from it what is known as
"a new man".'

James Bond got at any rate part of the message. As Mariko's
busy fingers proceeded to remove his trousers and then his
shirt, he lifted her chin and kissed her full on the soft, yielding,
bud-like mouth.

Later, sitting sweating and reflecting in the comfortable
wooden box, very tired, slightly, but cheerfully, drunk, he
remembered his dismal thoughts in Queen Mary's Rose
Garden. He also remembered his interview with M., and
M. saying that he could leave the hardware behind on this
purely diplomatic assignment; and the lines of irony round
Bond's mouth deepened.

Mariko was looking into the wall mirror and fiddling with
her hair and eyebrows. Bond said, 'Mariko. Out!'

Mariko smiled and bowed. She unhurriedly removed her
brassière and came towards the wooden box.

Bond reflected: What was it that Tiger had said about
becoming a new man? and he reached for Mariko's helping
hands and watched her breasts tauten as she pulled him out
and towards her.

It was indeed a new man who followed Tiger through the
thronged halls of Tokyo main station. Bond's face and
hands were of a light brown tint, his black hair, brightly
oiled, was cut and neatly combed in a short fringe that
reached halfway down his forehead, and the outer corners
of his eyebrows had been carefully shaved so that they now
slanted upwards. He was dressed, like so many of the other
travellers, in a white cotton shirt buttoned at the wrists and
a cheap, knitted silk, black tie exactly centred with a rolled
gold pin. His ready-made black trousers, held up by a cheap
black plastic belt, were rather loose in the fork, because Japanese behinds are inclined to hang low, but the black plastic
sandals and dark blue nylon socks were exactly the right size.
A much-used overnight bag of Japan Air Lines was slung

over his shoulder, and this contained a change of shirt, singlet, pants and socks, Shinsei cigarettes, and some cheap Japanese toilet articles. In his pockets were a comb, a cheap, used wallet containing some five thousand yen in small denomination notes, and a stout pocket knife which, by Japanese law, had a blade not more than two inches long. There was no handkerchief, only a packet of tissues. (Later, Tiger explained. 'Bondo-san, this Western habit of blowing the nose and carefully wrapping up the result in silk or fine linen and harbouring it in your pocket as if it were something precious! Would you do the same thing with the other excretions of your body? Exactly! So, if in Japan you wish to blow your nose, perform the act decorously and dispose at once, tidily, of the result.')

Despite his height, Bond merged quite adequately into the bustling, shoving crowd of passengers. His 'disguise' had mysteriously appeared in his room at the bathhouse and Mariko had greatly enjoyed dressing him up. 'Now Japanese gentleman,' she had said approvingly as, with a last lingering kiss, she had gone to answer Tiger's rap on the partition. Bond's own clothes and possessions had already been taken away.

'They and your things from the hotel will be transferred to Dikko's apartment,' Tiger had said. 'Later today, Dikko will inform your Chief that you have left Tokyo with me for a visit to the MAGIC establishment, which is, in fact, a day's journey from Tokyo, and that you will be away for several days. Dikko believes that this is so. My own department merely know that I shall be absent on a mission to Fukuoka. They do not know that you are accompanying me. And now we will take the express to Gamagori on the south coast and the evening hydrofoil across Ise Bay to the fishing port of Toba. There we will spend the night. This is to be a slow journey to Fukuoka for the purpose of training and educating you. It is necessary that I make you familiar with Japanese customs and folkways so that you make as few mistakes as possible – when the time comes.'

The gleaming orange and silver express slid to a stop beside them. Tiger barged his way on board. Bond waited politely for two or three women to precede him. When he sat down beside Tiger, Tiger hissed angrily, 'First lesson, Bondo-san! Do not make way for women. Push them, trample them down. Women have no priority in this country. You may be polite to very old men, but to no one else. Is that understood?'

'Yes, master,' said Bond sarcastically.

'And do not make Western-style jokes while you are my pupil. We are engaged on a serious mission.'

'Oh, all right, Tiger,' said Bond resignedly. 'But damn it all . . .'

Tiger held up a hand. 'And that is another thing. No swearing, please. There are no swear-words in the Japanese language and the usage of bad language does not exist.'

'But good heavens, Tiger! No self-respecting man could get through the day without his battery of four-letter words to cope with the roughage of life and let off steam. If you're late for a vital appointment with your superiors, and you find that you've left all your papers at home, surely you say, well, Freddie Uncle Charlie Katie, if I may put it so as not to offend.'

'No,' said Tiger. 'I would say "*Shimata*", which means "I have made a mistake".'

'Nothing worse?'

'There is nothing worse to say.'

'Well, supposing it was your driver's fault that the papers had been forgotten. Wouldn't you curse him backwards and sideways?'

'If I wanted to get myself a new driver, I might conceivably call him "*bakyaro*" which means a "bloody fool", or even "*konchikisho*" which means "you animal". But these are deadly insults and he would be within his rights to strike me. He would certainly get out of the car and walk away.'

'And those are the worst words in the Japanese language! What about your taboos? The Emperor, your ancestors, all these gods? Don't you ever wish them in hell, or worse?'

'No. That would have no meaning.'

'Well then, dirty words. Sex words?'

'There are two – "*chimbō*" which is masculine and "*mōnkō*" which is feminine. These are nothing but coarse anatomical descriptions. They have no meaning as swearing words. There are no such things in our language.'

'Well I'm . . . I mean, well I'm astonished. A violent people without a violent language! I must write a learned paper on this. No wonder you have nothing left but to commit suicide when you fail an exam, or cut your girl friend's head off when she annoys you.'

Tiger laughed. 'We generally push them under trams or trains.'

'Well, for my money, you'd do much better to say "You—",' Bond fired off the hackneyed string, 'and get it off your chest that way.'

'That is enough, Bondo-san,' said Tiger patiently. 'The subject is now closed. But you will kindly refrain both from using these words or looking them. Be calm, stoical, impassive. Do not show anger. Smile at misfortune. If you sprain your ankle, laugh.'

'Tiger, you're a cruel taskmaster.'

Tiger grinned with satisfaction. 'Bondo-san, you don't know the half of it. But now let us go and get something to eat and drink in the buffet car. All that Suntory you forced on me last night is crying out for the skin of the dog that bit me.'

'The hair,' corrected Bond.

'One hair would not be enough, Bondo-san. I need the whole skin.'

James Bond wrestled with his chopsticks and slivers of raw octopus and a mound of rice ('You must get accustomed to the specialities of the country, Bondo-san') and watched the jagged coastline, interspersed with glittering paddy-fields, flash by. He was lost in thought when he felt a hard jostle from behind. He had been constantly jostled as he sat up at the counter – the Japanese are great jostlers – but he now turned and caught a glimpse of the stocky back of a man disappearing into the next compartment. There were white strings round his ears which showed that he was wearing a *masko*, and he wore an ugly black leather hat. When they went back to their seat Bond found that his pocket had been picked. His wallet was gone. Tiger was astonished. 'That is very unusual in Japan,' he said defensively. 'But no matter. I will get you another at Toba. It would be a mistake to call the conductor. We do not wish to draw attention to ourselves. The police would be sent for at the next station and there would be much interrogation and filling out of forms. And there is no way of finding the thief. The man will have pocketed his *masko* and hat and will be unrecognizable. I regret the incident, Bondo-san. I hope you will forget it.'

'Of course. It's nothing.'

They left the train at Gamagori, a pretty seaside village with a humped island in the bay that Tiger said housed an important shrine, and the fifty-knot ride in the hydrofoil to Toba, an hour away across the bay, was exhilarating. As they disembarked, Bond caught a glimpse of a stocky silhouette in the crowd. Could it be the thief on the train? But the man wore heavy horn-rimmed spectacles, and there were many other stocky men in the crowd. Bond dismissed the thought and followed Tiger along the narrow streets, gaily hung with paper banners and lanterns, to the usual discreet frontage and dwarf pines that he had become accustomed to. They were expected and were greeted with deference. Bond had had about enough of the day. There weren't many bows and smiles left in him, and he was glad when he was at last left alone in his maddeningly dainty room with the usual dainty pot of tea, dainty cup and dainty sweetmeat wrapped in rice-paper. He sat at the open partition that gave on to a handkerchief of garden and then the sea wall and gazed gloomily across the water at a giant statue of a man in a bowler hat and morning coat that Tiger had told him was Mr Mikimoto, founder of the cultured pearl industry, who had been born at Toba and had there, as a poor fisherman, invented the trick of inserting grains of sand under the mantle of a live oyster to form the kernel of a pearl. Bond thought, To hell with Tiger and his crazy plan. What in God's name have I got myself into? He was still sitting there cursing his lot when Tiger came in and brusquely ordered him to don one of the *yukatas* that hung with the bedding in the single cupboard in the paper wall.

'You really must concentrate, Bondo-san,' said Tiger mildly. 'But you are making progress. As a reward I have ordered *sake* to be brought in large quantities and then a dinner of the speciality of this place, lobster.'

Bond's spirits rose minutely. He undressed to his pants, donned the dark-brown *yukata* ('Stop!' from Tiger. 'Wrap it round to the right! Only a corpse wraps it round to the left.') and adopted the lotus position across the low table from Tiger. He had to admit that the kimono was airy and comfortable. He bowed low. 'That sounds a most sincere programme. Now then, Tiger. Tell me about the time you were training as a *kami-kaze*. Every detail. What was it all about?'

The *sake* came. The pretty waitress knelt on the *tatami* and served them both. Tiger had been thoughtful. He had ordered tumblers. Bond swallowed his at one gulp. Tiger said, 'The grossness of your drinking habits fits well with your future identity.'

'And what is that to be?'

'A coalminer from Fukuoka. There are many tall men in that profession. Your hands are not rough enough, but you pushed a truck underground. Your nails will be filled with coal dust when the time comes. You were too stupid to wield a pick. You are deaf and dumb. Here,' Tiger slipped across a scrubby card, creased and dog-eared. There were some Japanese characters on it. 'That is "*Tsumbo de oshi*" – deaf and dumb. Your disability will inspire pity and some distaste. If someone talks to you, show that and they will desist. They may also give you a few pieces of small coin. Accept them and bow deeply.'

'Thanks very much. And I suppose I have to account for these tips to your secret fund?'

'That will not be necessary.' Tiger was wooden-faced. 'Our expenses on this mission are a direct charge on the Prime Minister's purse.'

Bond bowed. 'I am honoured.' He straightened himself.

'And now, you old bastard. More *sake* and tell me about the *kami-kaze*. In due course I am prepared to become a deaf and dumb miner from Fukuoka. In public I am prepared to hiss and bow with the best of them. But, by God, when we're alone, the password is Freddie Uncle Charlie Katie or I'll be putting my head under a pile-driver before you get me on to the first tee. Is that agreed?'

Tiger bowed low. '*Shimata*! I am in error. I have been pressing you hard. It is my duty to entertain a friend as well as instruct a pupil. Lift your glass, Bondo-san. Until you do so the girl will not pour. Right. Now you ask me about the *kami-kaze*.' Tiger rocked backwards and forwards and his dark, assassin's eyes became introspective. He didn't look up at Bond. He said, 'It was nearly twenty years ago. Things were looking bad for my country. I had been doing intelligence work in Berlin and Rome. I had been far from the air raids and even farther from the front line, and every night when I listened to the radio from my homeland and heard the bad news of the slow but sure approach of the American forces, island by island, airstrip by airstrip, I paid no attention to the false news of the Nazis, but thought only that my country was in danger and that I was needed to defend it.' Tiger paused. 'And the wine turned sour in my mouth and the girls turned cold in my bed. I listened to the accounts of this brilliant invention, the corps of *kami-kaze*. That is the "Divine Wind" that saved my country from invasion by Kublai Khan in the thirteenth century by destroying his fleet. I said to myself that that was the way to die – no medals, total death, suicide if you like, but at enormous cost to the enemy. It seemed to me the most heroic form of personal combat that had ever been invented. I was nearly forty. I had lived fully. It seemed to me that I could take the place of a younger man. The technique was simple. Anyone can learn to pilot a plane. The escorts of fighter planes led in to the attack. It was then just a question of aiming yourself at the largest ship, preferably an aircraft carrier that was bringing planes to the islands to attack the homeland. You got the ship lined up below you and you went for the flight deck and the lift which is the heart of a carrier. Pay no attention to the bridge or the water line. They are heavily armoured. Go for the vulnerable machinery of the flight deck. You understand?'

Tiger was completely sent. He was back there again fighting the war. Bond knew the symptoms. He often visited this haunted forest of memory himself. He lifted his glass. The kneeling girl bowed and poured. Bond said, 'Yes. Go on, Tiger.'

'I forced the Kempeitai to accept my resignation and I returned to Japan and more or less bribed my way into a *kami-kaze* training squadron. They were very difficult to get into. All the youth of the nation seemed to want to serve the Emperor in this way. At this time we were running out of aircraft and we were forced to use the more difficult *baku* – that was a small plane made mostly of wood with a thousand pounds of explosive in the nose, a kind of flying bomb. It had no engine, but was released from below the belly of a fighter bomber. The pilot had a single joystick for controlling direction.' Tiger looked up. 'I can tell you, Bondo-san, that it was a terrible and beautiful thing to see an attack wave going off. These young men in their pure white shifts, and with the ancient white scarf that was the badge of the *samurai* bound round their heads, running joyfully for their planes as if they were running to embrace a loved one. The roar of the engines of the mother planes, and then the take-off into the dawn or into the setting sun towards some distant target that had been reported by spies or intercepted on the radio. It was as if they were flying to their ancestors in heaven, as indeed they were, for of course none ever came back or were captured.'

'But what did it all achieve? Of course it frightened the American fleet all right, and the British. But you lost thousands of your best young men. Was it worth it?'

'Is it worth writing one of the most glorious pages in your country's history? Do you know that the *kami-kaze* is the only unit in the history of air warfare whose claims were less than the truth? The unit claimed as sunk or damaged 276 naval craft from aircraft carriers downwards. Those actually sunk or damaged were 322.'

'You were lucky the surrender came before you were sent on a mission.'

'Perhaps. And yet, Bondo-san, it is one of my most cherished dreams today to come diving out of the sun into a hail of anti-aircraft fire, see the tiny, terrified figures running for shelter from the flight deck of a wildly swerving carrier and know that you are about to kill a hundred or more of the enemy and destroy a million pounds' worth of his fighting machine, all by yourself.'

'And I suppose Admiral Ohnishi, who invented the whole idea, committed suicide when the surrender came?'

'Naturally. And in a most honourable fashion. When you commit *seppuku* you invite two of your best friends to be present to finish you off if you fail. The Admiral executed the cross-cut from left to right of the belly, and then the upward cut to the breast bone, most admirably. But it did not kill him. Yet he refused the *coup de grâce*. He sat there contemplating his insides for a whole day before he finally died. A most sincere gesture of apology to the Emperor.' Tiger waved a hand airily. 'However, I must not spoil your dinner. I can see that some of our honourable customs offend your soft Western susceptibilities. Here comes the lobster. Are they not splendid animals?'

Lacquer boxes of rice, raw quails' egg in sauce and bowls of sliced seaweed were placed in front of them both. Then they were each given a fine oval dish bearing a large lobster whose head and tail had been left as a dainty ornament to the sliced pink flesh in the centre. Bond set to with his chopsticks. He was surprised to find that the flesh was raw. He was even more surprised when the head of his lobster began moving off his dish and, with questing antennae and scrabbling feet, tottered off across the table. 'Good God, Tiger!' Bond said, aghast. 'The damn thing's alive!'

Tiger hissed impatiently, 'Really, Bondo-san. I am much disappointed in you. You fail test after test. I sincerely hope you will show improvement during the rest of our journey. Now eat up and stop being squeamish. This is a very great Japanese delicacy.'

James Bond bowed ironically. '*Shimata*!' he said. 'I have made a mistake. It crossed my mind that honourable Japanese lobster might not like being eaten alive. Thank you for correcting the unworthy thought.'

'You will soon become accustomed to the Japanese way of life,' said Tiger graciously.

'It's their way of death that's got me a little bit puzzled,' said Bond amiably, and he handed his glass to the kneeling waitress for more *sake* to give him strength to try the seaweed.

10

ADVANCED STUDIES

TIGER and Bond stood in the shade of the avenue of giant cryptomerias and observed the pilgrims, slung with cameras, who were visiting the famous Outer Shrine of Ise, the greatest temple to the creed of Shintoism. Tiger said, 'All right. You have observed these people and their actions. They have been saying prayers to the sun goddess. Go and say a prayer without drawing attention to yourself.'

Bond walked over the raked path and through the great wooden archway and joined the throng in front of the shrine. Two priests, bizarre in their red kimonos and black helmets, were watching. Bond bowed towards the shrine, tossed a coin on to the wire-netting designed to catch the offerings, clapped his hands loudly, bent his head in an attitude of prayer, clapped his hands again, bowed and walked out.

'You did well,' said Tiger. 'One of the priests barely glanced at you. The public paid no attention. You should perhaps have clapped your hands more loudly. It is to draw the attention of the goddess and your ancestors to your presence at the shrine. Then they will pay more attention to your prayer. What prayer did you in fact make?'

'I'm afraid I didn't make any, Tiger. I was concentrating on remembering the right sequence of motions.'

'The goddess will have noted that, Bondo-san. She will help you to concentrate still more in the future. Now we will go back to the car and proceed to witness another interesting ceremony in which you will take part.'

Bond groaned. In the parking place beyond the vast *torii* that guarded the entrance, chars-à-bancs were disgorging hordes of students while the conductresses shouted '*Awri, awri, awri*' and blew whistles to help the drivers of other chars-à-bancs to back in. The giggling girls were severely dressed in dark blue with black cotton stockings. The youths wore the handsome, high-collared black uniform of Japanese students. Tiger led the way through the middle of the crowd. When they emerged Tiger looked pleased. 'Did you notice anything, Bondo-san?'

'Only a lot of pretty girls. Rather too young for me.'

'Wrong. Yesterday many of them would have stared and giggled behind their hands and said "*gaijin*". Today you were not recognized as a foreigner. Your appearance is one thing, but your comportment has also improved. You exude more self-confidence. You are more at home.' Tiger gave his golden sunburst of a smile. 'The Tanaka system. It is not so foolish as you think.'

Wadakin, on the road across the mountains to the ancient capital of Kyoto, was a little upland hamlet without distinction. Tiger gave decisive orders to the driver of the hired car and they arrived at a tall, barn-like building in a back street. There was a strong smell of cattle and manure. The chief herdsman, as he turned out to be, greeted them. He had the apple cheeks and wise kindly eyes of his counterparts in Scotland and the Tyrol. Tiger had a long conversation with him. The man looked at Bond and his eyes twinkled. He bowed perfunctorily and led the way inside. It was cool out of the sun. There were rows of stalls in which vastly fat brown cows lay chewing the cud. A gay small dog was licking the muzzle of one of them and being occasionally given a lick in return. The herdsman lifted a barrier and said something to one of the cows which got unsteadily up on to legs that had become spindly through lack of exercise. It ambled unsteadily out into the sunshine and looked warily at Tiger and Bond. The herdsman hauled out a crate of beer bottles. He opened one and handed it to Bond. Tiger said peremptorily, 'Give it to the cow to drink.'

Bond took the bottle and walked boldly up to the cow who raised her head and opened her slavering jaws. Bond thrust the bottle between them and poured. The cow almost ate the bottle in its delight and ran its harsh tongue gratefully over Bond's hand. Bond stood his ground. He was getting used to Tiger's ploys by now, and he was determined to show at any rate an approximation of the *kami-kaze* spirit whatever test Tiger put him to.

The herdsman now handed Bond a bottle of what appeared to be water. Tiger said, 'This is *shochu*. It is a very raw gin. Fill your mouth with it and spray it over the back of the cow and then massage it into the cow's flesh.'

Bond guessed that Tiger hoped he would swallow some of the gin and choke. He closed his throat but lustily filled his mouth with the stuff, compressed his lips and blew hard so that the vapour from the stuff would not go up his nostrils. He wiped his hands across his lips that were already stinging with the harsh spirit and scrubbed energetically at the rough pelt. The cow bent her head in ecstasy . . . Bond stood back. 'Now what?' he said belligerently. 'What's the cow going to do for me?'

Tiger laughed and translated for the herdsman, who also laughed and looked at Bond with some respect. Money changed hands, and with much happy talk between Tiger and the herdsman and final bows they got back into the car and drove into the village, where they were welcomed into a shuttered and discreet restaurant, polished, spotless and blessedly deserted. Tiger ordered and they sat in wonderful Western chairs at a real table while the usual dimpling waitresses brought *sake*. Bond swallowed down his first flask at one long gulp to wash away the rasp of the gin. He said to Tiger, 'And now, what was that all about?'

Tiger looked pleased with himself. 'You are about to eat what it was all about – the finest, most succulent beef in the world. Kobe beef, but of a grade you wouldn't find in the most expensive restaurant in Tokyo. This herd is owned by a friend of mine. The herdsman was a good man, was he not? He feeds each of his cows four pints of beer a day and massages them with *shochu* as you did. They also receive a rich meal of oaten porridge. You like beef?'

'No,' said Bond stolidly. 'As a matter of fact, I don't.'

'That is unfortunate,' said Tiger, not looking as if it were. 'For what you are about to eat is the finest steak that will be eaten today anywhere outside the Argentine. And you have earned it. The herdsman was greatly impressed by your sincere performance with his cow.'

'And what does that prove?' said Bond sourly. 'And what honourable experience is awaiting me this afternoon?'

The steak came. It was accompanied by various succulent side-dishes, including a saucer of blood, which Bond refused. But the meat could be cut with a fork, and was indeed without equal in Bond's experience. Tiger, munching with gusto, answered Bond's question. 'I am taking you to one of the secret training establishments of my Service,' he said. 'It is not far from here, in the mountains, in an old fortified castle. It goes under the name of the "Central Mountaineering School". It arouses no comment in the neighbourhood, which is just as well, since it is here that my agents are trained in one of the arts most dreaded in Japan – *ninjutsu*, which is, literally, the art of stealth or invisibility. All the men you will see have already graduated in at least ten of the eighteen martial arts of *bushido*, or "ways of the warrior", and they are now learning to be *ninja*, or "stealers-in", which has for centuries been part of the basic training of spies and assassins and saboteurs. You will see men walk across the surface of water, walk up walls and across ceilings, and you will be shown equipment which makes it possible for them to remain submerged under water for a full day. And many other tricks besides. For of course, apart from physical dexterity, the *ninja* were never the superhumans they were built up to be in the popular imagination. But, nevertheless, the secrets of *ninjutsu* are still closely guarded today and are the property of two main schools, the Iga and

the Togakure, from which my instructors are drawn. I think
you will be interested and perhaps learn something yourself
at this place. I have never approved of agents carrying guns
and other obvious weapons. In China, Korea and Oriental
Russia, which are, so to speak, my main beats, the possession
of any offensive weapon on arrest would be an obvious confession of guilt. My men are expected to be able to kill
without weapons. All they may carry is a staff and a length
of thin chain which can be easily explained away. You
understand?'

'Yes, that makes sense. We have a similar commando training school for unarmed combat attached to Headquarters. But,
of course, your judo and karate are special skills requiring
years of practice. How high did you get in judo, Tiger?'

Tiger picked his teeth reminiscently. 'No higher than a
Black Belt of the Seventh Dan. I never graduated to a Red
Belt, which is from the Eighth to the Eleventh Dan. To do
so would have meant abandoning all other forms of activity.
And with what object? To be promoted to the Twelfth and
final Dan on my death? In exchange for spending the whole
of my life tumbling about in the Kodokan Academy in Tokyo?
No thank you. That is the ambition of a lunatic.' He smiled.
'No *sake*! No beautiful girls! Worse still, probably no opportunity in a whole lifetime to exercise my art in anger, to tackle
a robber or murderer with a gun, and get the better of him.
In the higher realms of judo, you are nothing but a mixture
between a monk and a ballet dancer. Not for me!'

Back on the open, dusty road some instinct made Bond
glance through the rear window between the dainty lace
blinds that are both the hall-mark of a truly sincere hired
car and a dangerous impediment to the driver's vision. Far
behind, there was a solitary motor-cyclist. Later when they
turned up a minor road into the mountains, he was still there.
Bond mentioned the fact. Tiger shrugged. 'He is perhaps a
speed cop. If he is anyone else, he has chosen a bad time and
place.'

The castle was the usual horned roof affair of Japanese
prints. It stood in a cleft between the mountains that must

have once been an important pass, for ancient cannon pointed out from the summit of giant, slightly sloping walls of black granite blocks. They were stopped at the gate to a wooden causeway across a brimming moat and again at the castle entrance. Tiger showed his pass, and there was much hissing and deep bowing from the plain-clothes guards and a bell clanged in the topmost tier of the soaring edifice, which, as Bond could see from the inner courtyard, was badly in need of a coat of paint. As the car came to a stop young men in shorts and gym shoes came running from various doors in the castle and formed up behind three older men. They bowed almost to the ground as Tiger descended regally from the car. Tiger and Bond also bowed. Brief greetings were exchanged with the older men and Tiger then proceeded to fire off a torrent of staccato Japanese which was punctuated by respectful 'Hai's' from the middle-aged man who was obviously the commandant of the team. With a final 'Hai, Tanaka-san' this official turned to the twenty-odd students whose ages seemed to be somewhere between twenty-five and thirty-five. He called numbers and six men fell out of the ranks. They were given orders and ran off into the castle. Tiger commented to Bond. 'They will put on camouflage clothes and go off into the mountains through which we have come. If anyone is lurking about they will bring him to us. And now we will see a little demonstration of an attack on the castle.' Tiger fired off some more orders, the men dispersed at the double and Bond followed Tiger out on to the causeway accompanied by the chief instructor with whom Tiger had a long and animated discussion. Perhaps a quarter of an hour later, there came a whistle from above them on the ramparts and at once ten men broke cover from the forest to their left. They were dressed from head to foot in some black material, and only their eyes showed through slits in the black hoods. They ran down to the edge of the moat, donned oval battens of what must have been some light wood such as balsa, and skimmed across the water with a kind of skiing motion until they reached the bottom of the giant black wall. There they discarded their battens, took lengths of rope and a handful of small iron pitons out of pockets in their black robes and proceeded to almost run up the walls like fast black spiders.

Tiger turned to Bond. 'You understand that it is night-time. In a few days, you will have to be doing something similar. Note that the lengths of rope terminate in an iron hook which they throw up and catch in crevices between the stone blocks.' The instructor said something to Tiger and pointed. Tiger nodded. He said to Bond, 'The man at the end is the weakest of the team. The instructor thinks he will soon fall.'

The line of climbing men was now almost at the summit of the two-hundred-foot wall, and sure enough, with only yards to go, the end man lost his foothold and, with arms and legs flailing, and with a scream of terror, fell back down the sheer black face. His body hit once and then crashed into the calm waters of the moat. The instructor muttered something, stripped off his shirt, clambered on to the rail of the causeway and dived the hundred feet down into the water. It was a perfect dive, and he swam in a swift crawl towards the body that lay ominously face downwards in the moat. Tiger turned to Bond. 'It is of no account. He was going to fail the man anyway. And now come into the courtyard. The invaders have scaled the wall and they will now use *bojutsu* on the defenders, that is fighting with the stave.'

Bond took a last glance at the instructor, who was now towing the corpse, which it certainly was, to the shore by its black hood. Bond wondered if any of the students was going to fail his test at *bojutsu*. Failure was certainly total in Tiger's training camp!

Back in the courtyard, individual couples, dancing and dodging, were fighting furious single combats with thick staves about two yards long. They swung and parried with two hands on the stave, lunged at the belly, using the stave as a lance, or did complicated in-fighting with face almost pressed against face. Bond was astonished to see tremendous thrusts and whacks into the groin leaving the victim un-moved when he, Bond, would have been writhing in agony. He asked Tiger about this. Tiger, his eyes bright with the lust of battle, answered briefly that he would explain this later.

Meanwhile, the invaders were slowly being overcome by the defence. Black figures toppled unconscious or lay groaning with hands clutched to head or stomach or shin. Then there came a shrill blast on the whistle from one of the instructors, and it was all over. The defenders had won. A doctor appeared and attended the fallen, and those who were on their feet bowed deeply to one another and then in the direction of Tiger. Tiger made a brief and fierce speech which he later told Bond was of congratulation on the sincerity of the display, and Bond was then led into the castle to drink tea and view the museum of *ninja* armament. This included spiked steel wheels, the size of a silver dollar, which could be whirled on the finger and thrown, chains with spiked weights at each end, used like the South American bolas for catching cattle, sharp nails twisted into knots for defeating barefoot pursuers (Bond remembered similar devices spread on the roads by the Resistance to puncture the tyres of German staff cars), hollowed bamboo for breathing under water (Bond had used the same device during an adventure on a Caribbean island), varieties of brass knuckles, gloves whose palms were studded with very sharp, slightly hooked nails for 'walking' up walls and across ceilings, and a host of similar rather primitive gadgets of offence and defence. Bond made appropriate noises of approval and amazement and reflected on the comparable Russian invention used with much success in West Germany, a cyanide gas pistol that left no trace and a sure diagnosis of heart failure. Tiger's much vaunted *ninjutsu* just wasn't in the same league!

Out in the courtyard again, the leader of the camouflaged troop reported the discovery of motor-cycle tyre tracks that stopped and turned back a mile from the castle. That had been the only trace of a tail. Then came, to Bond, the blessed bows and farewells and they were on their way again, bound for Kyoto.

'Well, Bondo-san. What did you think of my training school?'

'I thought it was very sincere. I can imagine that the skills that are learned would be most valuable, but I would have

thought that the black dress for night work and the various
gadgets would have been as incriminating, if you were caught,
as a pistol. But they certainly went up that wall damned quick,
and that *bojutsu* business would be very effective against the
usual night-prowler with a bicycle chain or a flick knife. I
must get Swaine and Adeney to make me a two-yard-long
walking stick.'

Tiger sucked his teeth impatiently. 'You speak like a man
who only knows of the sort of fighting that goes on in a
cheap Western. You would not get very far with your methods
if you were trying to penetrate North Korea dressed as a
simple peasant with his staff.'

James Bond was rather exhausted by the day. He was also
sorry for the student who had died showing off for his and
Tiger's delectation. He said shortly, 'None of your *ninjas* would
last very long in East Berlin,' and relapsed into a surly silence.

11

ANATOMY CLASS

To Bond's unspeakable relief, they put up that night at the
smartest hotel in Kyoto, the Miyako. The comfortable bed,
air-conditioning and Western-style lavatory on which one
could actually sit were out of this world. Better still, Tiger
said that unfortunately he had to dine with the Chief of Police
of the prefecture and Bond ordered a pint of Jack Daniels and
a double portion of eggs Benedict to be brought up to his
room. Then, from a belated sense of duty, he watched 'The
Seven Detectives', a famous Japanese television series, failed
to spot the villain, and went to bed and slept for twelve
hours.

The next morning, hungover and conscience-stricken, he
obediently fell in with Tiger's plans that they should visit the
oldest whore-house in Japan before a quick drive to Osaka
for the day's journey across the Inland Sea to the southern

island of Kyūshū. 'Bit early for visiting a whore-house,' had been his only comment.

Tiger laughed. 'It is a matter of deep regret to me that your baser instincts should always be in the ascendancy, Bondo-san. Prostitution is now illegal in Japan. What we are about to visit is a national monument.'

'Oh, good show!'

There was a deal of bowing and hissing at the whore-house, a spacious establishment in the now defunct red lamp street of the ancient capital, and they were presented with handsomely bound descriptive booklets by the earnest curator. They wandered over polished floors from chamber to chamber, and gravely inspected the sword cuts in the wooden supports that had been inflicted, according to Tiger, by *samurai* infuriated by lust and impatience. Bond inquired how many actual bedrooms there had been. It seemed to him that the whole place was taken up by a vast kitchen and many diningrooms.

'Four rooms,' answered the curator.

'That's no way to run a whore-house,' commented Bond. 'You need quick throughput, like a casino.'

'Bondo-san,' complained Tiger. 'Please try and put out of your mind comparisons between our way of life and yours. In former times, this was a place of rest and recreation. Food was served and there was music and story-telling. People would write *tankas*. Take that inscription on the wall. It says "Everything is new tomorrow." Some man with a profound mind will have written that.'

'Then he threw his pen away and reached for his sword and shouted, "When is room No. 4 going to be empty?" National monument indeed! It's like in the new African States where they pretend the cannibal stewpot in the chief's hut was for cooking yams for the hungry children. Everyone tries to forget his rowdy past instead of being proud of it. Like we are of Bloody Morgan, or Nell Gwynne, for instance. The great murderer and the great whore are part of our history. You shouldn't try and pretend that your oldest whore-house is a sort of Stratford-on-Avon.'

Tiger uttered an explosive laugh. 'Bondo-san, your comments on our Japanese way of life become more and more outrageous. Come, it is time to cleanse your mind in the salubrious breezes of the Inland Sea.'

The *Murasaki Maru* was a very modern 3,000-ton ship with all the luxuries of an ocean liner. Crowds waved her goodbye as if the ship was setting off across the Atlantic instead of doing a day trip down the equivalent of a long lake. There was much throwing of paper streamers by groups bearing placards to show whom they represented – business outings, schools, clubs – part of the vast travelling population of Japan, for ever on the move, making an outing, visiting relatives or shrines, or just seeing the sights of the country. The ship throbbed grandly through the endless horned islands. Tiger said that there were fine whirlpools 'like great lavatory pans, specially designed for suicides' between some of these. Meanwhile, Tiger and Bond sat in the first class dining-room and consumed 'Hamlets' – ham omelets – and *sake*. Tiger was in a lecturing mood. He was determined to correct Bond's boorish ignorance of Japanese culture. 'Bondo-san, I wonder if I will ever get you to appreciate the nuances of the Japanese *tanka*, or of the *haiku*, which are the classical forms of Japanese verse. Have you ever heard of Bashō, for instance?'

'No,' said Bond with polite interest. 'Who's he?'

'Just so,' said Tiger bitterly. 'And yet you would think me grossly uneducated if I had never heard of Shakespeare, Homer, Dante, Cervantes, Goethe. And yet Bashō, who lived in the seventeenth century, is the equal of any of them.'

'What did he write?'

'He was an itinerant poet. He was particularly at home with the *haiku*, the verse of seventeen syllables.' Tiger assumed a contemplative expression. He intoned:

> 'In the bitter radish
> that bites into me, I feel
> the autumn wind.

'Does that not say anything to you? Or this:

'The butterfly is perfuming
its wings, in the scent
of the orchid.

'You do not grasp the beauty of that image?'
'Rather elusive compared to Shakespeare.'

'In the fisherman's hut
mingled with dried shrimps
crickets are chirping.'

Tiger looked at him hopefully.

'Can't get the hang of that one,' said Bond apologetically.

'You do not catch the still-life quality of these verses? The flash of insight into humanity, into nature? Now, do me a favour, Bondo-san. Write a *haiku* for me yourself. I am sure you could get the hang of it. After all you must have had *some* education?'

Bond laughed. 'Mostly in Latin and Greek. All about Caesar and Balbus and so on. Absolutely no help in ordering a cup of coffee in Rome or Athens after I'd left school. And things like trigonometry, which I've totally forgotten. But give me a pen and a piece of paper and I'll have a bash, if you'll forgive the bad joke.' Tiger handed them over and Bond put his head in his hands. Finally, after much crossing out and rewriting he said, 'Tiger, how's this? It makes just as much sense as old Bashō and it's much more pithy.' He read out:

'You only live twice:
Once when you are born
And once when you look death in the face.'

Tiger clapped his hands softly. He said with real delight, 'But that is excellent, Bondo-san. Most sincere.' He took the pen and paper and jotted some ideograms up the page. He shook his head. 'No, it won't do in Japanese. You have the wrong number of syllables. But it is a most honourable attempt.' He looked keenly at Bond. 'You were perhaps thinking of your mission?'

'Perhaps,' said Bond with indifference.

'It is weighing on your mind?'

'The practical difficulties are bound to do so. I have swallowed the moral principles involved. Things being as they are, I have to accept that the end justifies the means.'

'Then you are not concerned with your own safety?'

'Not particularly. I've had worse jobs to do.'

'I must congratulate you on your stoicism. You do not appear to value your life as highly as most Westerners.' Tiger looked at him kindly. 'Is there perhaps a reason for that?'

Bond was offhand. 'Not that I can think of. But for God's sake chuck it, Tiger! None of your Japanese brain-washing! More *sake*, and answer my question of yesterday. Why weren't those men disabled by those terrific slashes to the groin? That might be of some practical value to me instead of all this waffle about poetry.'

Tiger ordered the *sake*. He laughed. 'Unfortunately you are too old to benefit. I would need to have caught you at the age of about fourteen. You see, it is this way. You know the *sumo* wrestlers? It is they who invented the trick many centuries ago. It is vital for them to be immune from damage to those parts of the body. Now, you know that, in men, the testicles, which until puberty have been held inside the body, are released by a particular muscle and descend between the legs?'

'Yes.'

'Well the *sumo* wrestler will have been selected for his profession by the time of puberty. Perhaps because of his weight and strength, or perhaps because he comes of a *sumo* family. Well, by assiduously massaging those parts, he is able, after much practice, to cause the testicles to re-enter the body up the inguinal canal down which they originally descended.'

'My God, you Japanese!' said Bond with admiration. 'You really are up to all the tricks. You mean he gets them right out of the way behind the bones of the pelvis or what not?'

'Your knowledge of anatomy is as vague as your appreciation for poetry, but that is more or less so, yes. Then, before a fight, he will bind up that part of the body most thoroughly to contain these vulnerable organs in their hiding-place. Afterwards, in the bath, he will release them to hang normally. I have seen them do it. It is a great pity that it is now too late for you to practise this art. It might have given you more confidence on your mission. It is my experience that agents fear most for that part of the body when there is fighting to be done or when they risk capture. These organs, as you know, are most susceptible to torture for the extraction of information.'

'Don't I know it!' said Bond from the heart. 'Some of our chaps wear a box when they think they're in for a rough house. I don't care for them. Too uncomfortable.'

'What is a box?'

'It is what our cricketers wear to protect those parts when they go out to bat. It is a light padded shield of aluminium.'

'I regret that we have nothing of that nature. We do not play cricket in Japan. Only baseball.'

'Lucky for you you weren't occupied by the British,' commented Bond. 'Cricket is a much more difficult and skilful game.'

'The Americans say otherwise.'

'Naturally. They want to sell you baseball equipment.'

They arrived at Beppu in the southern island of Kyūshū as the sun was setting. Tiger said that this was just the time to see the famous geysers and fumaroles of the little spa. In any case, there would be no time in the morning as they would have to start early for Fukuoka, their final destination. Bond shivered slightly at the name. The moment was rapidly approaching when the *sake* and sightseeing would have to stop.

Above the town of Beppu, they visited in turn the ten spectacular 'hells' as they are officially designated. The stink of sulphur was disgusting, and each bubbling, burping nest of volcanic fumaroles was more horrific than the last. The steaming mud and belching geysers were of different colours – red, blue, and orange – and everywhere there were warning notices and skulls and crossbones to keep visitors at a safe distance. The tenth 'hell' announced in English and Japanese that there would be an eruption punctually every twenty minutes. They joined a small group of spectators under the arc lights that pinpointed a small quiescent crater in a rock area bespattered with mud. Sure enough, in five minutes, there came a rumbling from underground and a jet of steaming grey mud shot twenty feet up into the air and splashed down inside the enclosure. As Bond was turning away, he noticed a large red painted wheel, heavily padlocked and surrounded by wire-netting in a small separate enclosure. There were warning notices above it and a particularly menacing skull and crossbones. Bond asked Tiger what it was.

'It says that this wheel controls the pulse of the geyser. It says that if this wheel were screwed down it could result in the destruction of the entire establishment. It gives the explosive force of the volcano, if the exhaust valve of the geyser were to be closed, as the equivalent of a thousand pounds of TNT. It is, of course, all a bit of nonsense to attract the tourists. But now, back to the town, Bondo-san! Since it is our last day together,' he added hastily, 'on this particular voyage, I have arranged a special treat. I ordered it by radio from the ship. A *fugu* feast!'

Bond cursed silently. The memory of his eggs Benedict the night before was intolerably sweet. What new monstrosity was this? he asked.

'*Fugu* is the Japanese blow-fish. In the water, it looks like a brown owl, but when captured it blows itself up into a ball covered with wounding spines. We sometimes dry the skins and put candles inside and use them as lanterns. But the flesh is particularly delicious. It is the staple food of the *sumo* wrestlers because it is supposed to be very strength-giving. The fish is also very popular with suicides and murderers because its liver and sex glands contain a poison which brings death instantaneously.'

'That's just what I would have chosen for dinner. How thoughtful of you, Tiger.'

'Have no fear, Bondo-san. Because of the dangerous properties of the fish, every *fugu* restaurant has to be manned by experts and be registered with the State.'

They left their bags at a Japanese inn where Tiger had reserved rooms, enjoyed the *o-furo*, honourable bath, together in the blue-tiled miniature swimming pool whose water was very hot and smelled of sulphur and then, totally relaxed, went off down the street leading to the sea.

(Bond had become enamoured of the civilized, vaguely Roman, bathing habits of the Japanese. Was it because of these, because they washed *outside* the bath instead of wallowing in their own effluvia, that they all smelled so clean? Tiger said bluntly that, at the very best, Westerners smelled of sweet pork.)

The restaurant had a giant blow-fish hanging as a sign above the door, and inside, to Bond's relief, there were Western-style chairs and tables at which a smattering of people were eating with the intense concentration of the Japanese. They were expected and their table had been prepared. Bond said, 'Now then, Tiger, I'm not going to commit honourable suicide without at least five bottles of *sake* inside me.' The flasks were brought, all five of them, to the accompaniment of much tittering by the waitresses. Bond downed the lot, tumbler by tumbler, and expressed himself satisfied. 'Now you can bring on this blasted blow-fish,' he said belligerently, 'and if it kills me it will be doing a good turn to our friend the doctor in his castle.'

A very beautiful white porcelain dish as big as a bicycle wheel was brought forward with much ceremony. On it were arranged, in the pattern of a huge flower, petal upon petal of a very thinly sliced and rather transparent white fish. Bond followed Tiger's example and set to with his chopsticks. He was proud of the fact that he had reached Black Belt standard with these instruments – the ability to eat an underdone fried egg with them.

The fish tasted of nothing, not even of fish. But it was very pleasant on the palate and Bond was effusive in his compliments because Tiger, smacking his lips over each morsel, obviously expected it of him. There followed various side-dishes containing other parts of the fish, and more *sake*, but this time containing raw *fugu* fins.

Bond sat back and lit a cigarette. He said, 'Well, Tiger. This is nearly the end of my education. Tomorrow you say I am to leave the nest. How many marks out of a hundred?'

Tiger looked at him quizzically. 'You have done well, Bondo-san. Apart from your inclination to make Western jokes about Eastern customs. Fortunately I am a man of infinite patience, and I must admit that your company has given me much pleasure and a certain amount of amusement. I will award you seventy-five marks out of a possible hundred.'

As they rose to go, a man brushed past Bond to get to the exit. He was a stocky man with a white *masko* over his mouth and he wore an ugly leather hat. The man on the train!

Well, well! thought Bond. If he shows up on the last lap to Fukuoka, I'll get him. If not I'll reluctantly put it down to 'Funny Coincidence Department'. But it looks like nought out of a hundred to Tiger for powers of observation.

Part Two

**. . . than
to
arrive'**

12

APPOINTMENT IN SAMARA

AT SIX in the morning, a car from the Prefect of Police in Fukuoka came for them. There were two police corporals in the front seat. They went off northwards on the coast road at a good pace. After a while, Bond said, 'Tiger, we're being followed. I don't care what you say. The man who stole my wallet was in the *fugu* restaurant last night, and he's now a mile behind on a motor-cycle – or I'll eat my hat. Be a good chap and tell the driver to dodge up a side-road and then go after him and get him. I've got a sharp nose for these things and I ask you to do what I say.'

Tiger grunted. He looked back and then issued rapid instructions to the driver. The driver said, '*Hai!*' briskly, and the corporal at his side unbuttoned the holster of his M-14 automatic. Tiger flexed his powerful fingers.

They came to a track on the left which went into the scrub. The driver did a good racing change and pulled in out of sight of the road. He cut his engine. They listened. The roar of a motor-cycle approached and receded. The driver reversed sharply on to the road and tore off in pursuit. Tiger issued more sharp instructions. He said to Bond, 'I have told him to try warning the man with his siren and if he doesn't stop to ride him into the ditch.'

'Well, I'm glad you're giving him a chance,' said Bond, beginning to have qualms. 'I may be wrong and he may only be a Fuller brush man in a hurry.'

They were doing eighty along the winding road. They soon came up with the man's dust and then there was the machine itself. The man was hunched over the handlebars, going like hell.

The driver said something. Tiger translated, 'He says it's a 500 c.c. Honda. On that, he could easily get away from us.

But even Japanese crooks are men of discipline. He will prefer to obey the siren.'

The siren wailed and then screamed. The white mask gleamed as the man glanced over his shoulder. He braked slowly to a stop. His right hand went inside his jacket. Bond had his hand on the door-latch. He said, 'Watch out, Tiger, he's got a gun!' and, as they pulled up alongside, he hurled himself out of the door and crashed into the man, knocking him and his machine to the ground. The corporal beside the driver took a flying leap and the two bodies rolled into the ditch. Almost immediately the corporal got to his feet. He had a blood-stained knife in his hand. He threw it aside and tore at the man's coat and shirt. He looked up and shook his head. Tiger shouted something and the corporal began slapping the man's face as hard as he could from side to side. The *masko* was knocked off and Bond recognized the snarling rictus of death. He said, sickened, 'Stop him, Tiger! The man's dead.'

Tiger walked down into the ditch. He picked up the man's knife and bent down and slit the right sleeve of the corpse up to the shoulder. He looked and then called Bond down. He pointed to a black ideogram tattooed in the crook of the man's arm. He said, 'You were right, Bondo-san. He is a Black Dragon.' He stood up and, his face contorted, spat out: '*Shimata!*'

The two policemen were standing by looking politely baffled. Tiger gave them orders. They searched the man's clothing and extracted various commonplace objects including Bond's wallet, with the five thousand yen still intact, and a cheap diary. They handed everything to Tiger and then hauled the corpse out of the ditch and stuffed it roughly into the boot of the car. Then they hid the motor-cycle in some bushes and everyone dusted themselves and got back into the car.

After a few moments, Tiger said thoughtfully, 'It is incredible! These people must have a permanent tail on me in Tokyo.' He riffled through the diary. 'Yes, all my movements for the past week and all the stopping-places on our journey. You are simply described as a *gaijin*. But he could have telephoned a description. This is indeed an unfortunate business, Bondo-san. I apologize most deeply. You may already be incriminated. I will naturally absolve you from your mission. It is entirely my fault for being careless. I have not been taking these people seriously enough. I must talk with Tokyo as soon as we get to Fukuoka. But at least you have seen an example of the measures Doctor Shatterhand takes for his protection. There is certainly more to this man than meets the eye. At some time in his life he must have been an experienced intelligence agent. To have discovered my identity, for instance, which is a State secret. To have recognized me as his chief enemy. To have taken the appropriate counter-measures to ensure his privacy. This is either a great madman or a great criminal. You agree, Bondo-san?'

'Looks mighty like it. I'm really getting quite keen to have a sight of the fellow. And don't worry about the mission. This was probably just the jolt I needed to get the wind under my tail.'

The headquarters of the local department of the Sosaka, the CID, for the southern island of Kyūshū, was just off the main street of Fukuoka. It was a stern-looking building in yellow lavatory brick in a style derived from the German. Tiger confirmed that it had been the headquarters of the Kempeitai, the Japanese Gestapo, before and during the war. Tiger was received with pomp. The office of the Chief of the CID was small and cluttered. Superintendent Ando himself looked to Bond like any other Japanese salary-man, but he had a military bearing and the eyes behind the rimless spectacles were quick and hard. Bond sat patiently smoking while much conversation went on. A blown-up aerial mosaic of the Castle of Death and the surrounding country was produced from a filing cabinet and laid out on the desk. Superintendent Ando weighed down the corners with ashtrays and other hardware and Tiger called him over with a respect, Bond noticed, that was not lost on the Superintendent. It crossed Bond's mind that he had heaped much ON on Tiger, or alternatively that Tiger had lost much face *vis-à-vis* Bond by the business of the Black Dragon agent. Tiger said, 'Please to examine this photograph, Bondo-san. The Superintendent says that a clandestine approach from the landward side is now very difficult. The suicides pay local peasants to lead them through these marshlands,' he pointed, 'and there are recognized breaches in the walls surrounding the property which are constantly changed and kept open for the suicides. Every time the Superintendent posts a guard at one of them, another is made known to the peasants by the castle guards. He says he is at his wits' end. Twenty bodies have been fetched to the mortuary in the past week. The Superintendent wishes to hand in his resignation.'

'Naturally,' said Bond. 'And then perhaps honourable *fugu* poisoning. Let's have a look.'

At first glance, Bond's heart quailed. He might just as well try and storm Windsor Castle single-handed! The estate covered the whole expanse of a small promontory that jutted out into the sea from a rocky coast, and the two-hundred-foot cliff round the promontory had been revetted with giant stone blocks down to the breaking waves to form an unbroken wall that sloped slightly up to gun-ports and the irregularly-sited, tiled watch-towers. From the top of this wall there appeared to be a ten-foot drop into the park, heavily treed and shrubbed between winding streams and a broad lake with a small island in its centre. Steam appeared to be rising from the lake and there were occasional wisps of it among the shrubbery. At the back of the property stood the castle, protected from the low-lying countryside by a comparatively modest wall. It would be over this wall that the suicides gained access. The castle itself was a giant five-storeyed affair in the Japanese tradition, with swooping, winged roofs of glazed tile. Dolphin-shaped finials decorated the topmost storey, and there was a profusion of other decorative devices, small balconies, isolated turrets and gazebos so that the whole black-painted edifice, edged here and there with what Tiger said was gold paint, gave the impression of a brilliant attempt to make a stage setting for Dracula. Bond picked up a large magnifying glass and ran over the whole property inch by inch, but there was nothing more to be gleaned except the presence of an occasional diminutive figure at work in the park or raking the gravel round the castle.

Bond laid down the glass. He said gloomily, 'That's not a castle! That's a fortress! How am I supposed to get into the bloody place?'

'The Superintendent asks if you are a good swimmer. I have had a complete outfit sent down from my *ninjutsu* establishment. The seaward wall would present no problems.'

'I can swim well enough, but how do I get to the base of the wall? Where do I start from?'

'The Superintendent says there is an Ama island called Kuro only half a mile out to sea.'

'What's an Ama island?'

'They exist at different places round Japan. I believe there are some fifty such settlements. The Ama are a tribe whose girls dive for the *awabi* shells – that is our local abalone. A clam. It is a great delicacy. They sometimes dive for pearl oysters. They dive naked. Some of them are very beautiful. But they keep themselves very much to themselves and visitors to their islands are completely discouraged. They have their own primitive culture and customs. I suppose you could compare them to sea-gipsies. They rarely marry outside the tribe, and it is that which has made them a race apart.'

'Sounds intriguing, but how am I going to make a base on this Kuro Island? I may have to wait days for the weather to be right.'

Tiger spoke rapidly to the Superintendent and there was a lengthy reply. '*Ah, so desu ka!*' said Tiger with interest and enthusiasm. He turned to Bond. 'It seems that the Superintendent is distantly related to a family on Kuro. It is a most interesting family. There is a father and a mother and one daughter. She is called Kissy Suzuki. I have heard of her. When she was seventeen, she became famous in Japan by being chosen to go to Hollywood to make a film. They wanted a Japanese diving girl of great beauty and someone had heard of her. She made the film, but hated Hollywood and longed only to return to her Ama life. She could have made a fortune, but she retired to this obscure island. There was a great to-do in the Press at the time, and it was judged that she had behaved most honourably. They christened her "The Japanese Garbo". But Kissy will now be twenty-three and everyone has forgotten about her. The Superintendent says that he could arrange for you to stay with this family. They seem to have some obligation towards him. He says it is a simple house, but comfortable because of the money this girl earned in Hollywood. The other houses on the island are nothing but fishermen's shacks.'

'But won't the rest of the community resent me being there?'

'No. The people of the island belong to the Shinto religion. The Superintendent will speak to the Shinto priest and everything will be okay.'

'All right, so I stay on this island and then one night I swim across to the wall. How do I get up it?'

'You will have the *ninja* outfit. It is here. You have seen how it is used. You will use it. It is very simple.'

'As I saw from the man who fell into the moat. Then what do I do?'

'You hide up in the grounds and wait for an opportunity to kill him. How you do that is up to you. As I told you, he goes about in armour. A man in armour is very vulnerable. You only have to knock him off his feet. Then you will throttle him with the *ninja* chain you will be wearing round your waist. If his wife is with him, you will throttle her too. She is certainly involved in all this business, and anyway she is too ugly to live. Then you escape over the wall and swim back to Kuro. There you will be picked up by the police launch which will visit the place at once. The news of the death will quickly get round.'

Bond said doubtfully, 'Well, it all sounds very simple. But what about these guards? The place is crawling with them.'

'You must just keep out of their way. As you can see, the park is full of hiding-places.'

'Thanks very much. In one of those poison bushes or up one of those trees. I don't want to blind myself or go mad.'

'The *ninja* clothing will give you complete protection. You will have a black suit for night and a camouflage one for the day. You will wear the swimming goggles to protect your eyes. All this equipment you will tow over in a plastic bag which will be provided.'

'My dear Tiger, you've thought of everything. But I'd much rather have just one little gun.'

'That would be crazy, Bondo-san. You know perfectly well that silence will be essential. And with a silencer, which would be very heavy to swim with, the speed of the bullet would be so much reduced that you might not pierce the armour. No, my friend. Use *ninjutsu*. It is the only way.'

'Oh, all right,' said Bond resignedly. 'Now let's have a look at a photograph of this chap. Has the Superintendent got one?'

It had been taken from a long way away with a telephoto lens. It showed a giant figure in full medieval chain armour with the jagged, winged helmet of ancient Japanese warriors. Bond studied the photograph carefully, noting the vulnerable spots at neck and joints. A metal shield protected the man's groin. A wide-bladed *samurai* sword hung from his waist, but there was no sign of any other weapon. Bond said thoughtfully, 'He doesn't look as daft as he ought to. Probably because of the Dracula setting. Have you got one of his face? Perhaps he looks a bit madder in the raw.'

The Superintendent went to the bottom of his file and extracted what looked like a blown-up copy of Doctor Guntram Shatterhand's passport photograph and handed it over.

Bond took it nonchalantly. Then his whole body stiffened. He said to himself, God Almighty! God Almighty! Yes. There was no doubt, no doubt at all! He had grown a drooping black moustache. He had had the syphilitic nose repaired. There was a gold-capped tooth among the upper frontals, but there could be no doubt. Bond looked up. He said, 'Have you got one of the woman?'

Startled by the look of controlled venom on Bond's face, and by the pallor that showed through the walnut dye, the Superintendent bowed energetically and scrabbled through his file.

Yes, there she was, the bitch – the flat, ugly wardress face, the dull eyes, the scraped-back bun of hair.

Bond held the pictures, not looking at them, thinking.

Ernst Stavro Blofeld. Irma Bunt. So this was where they had come to hide! And the long, strong gut of fate had lassoed him to them! They of all people! He of all people! A taxi-ride down the coast in this remote corner of Japan. Could they smell him coming? Had the dead spy got hold of his name and told them? Unlikely. The power and prestige of Tiger would have protected him. Privacy, discretion, are the heartbeat of Japanese inns. But would they know that an enemy was on his way? That fate had arranged this appointment in Samara? Bond looked up from the pictures. He was in cold control of himself. This was now a private matter. It had nothing to do with Tiger or Japan. It had nothing to do with MAGIC 44. It was ancient feud. He said casually, 'Tiger, could the Superintendent inquire what his detectives have made of that Black Dragon agent? And of his belongings? I am particularly interested to know whether he may have telephoned or telegraphed my description or my purpose in coming down here.'

There was a long and electric silence in the room. Tiger examined Bond's face with piercing interest before he passed the inquiry on to the Superintendent. The Superintendent picked up the receiver of an old-fashioned telephone on a double hook. He spoke into it, then, a Japanese habit, blew sharply into the mouthpiece to clear the line, and spoke again at length. He said, '*Ah, so desu ka!*' many times. Then he put down the receiver. When he had finished talking, Tiger turned to Bond. Again with the same piercing appraisal of Bond's face, he said, 'The man came from these parts. He has a police record. Fortunately, he was poorly educated and is known as nothing more than a stupid thug. On the first page of the diary he wrote down his assignment, which was only to follow me to my destination and then report to his master. It seems unlikely that he was provided with funds for expensive communications. But what is it, Bondo-san? Is it that you know these people?'

James Bond laughed. It was a laugh that grated. Even to Bond, it sounded harsh and false in the small room. He had immediately made up his mind to keep his knowledge to himself. To reveal the true identity of Doctor Shatterhand would be to put the whole case back into official channels. The Japanese Secret Service and the CIA would swarm down to Fukuoka. Blofeld and Irma Bunt would be arrested. James Bond's personal prey would be snatched from him. There would be no revenge! Bond said, 'Good lord, no! But I am something of a physiognomist. When I saw this man's face, it was as if someone had walked over my grave. I have a feeling that, whether I succeed or not, the outcome of this mission is going to be decisive for one or the other of us. It will not be a drawn game. But now I have a number of further questions with which I must worry you and the Superintendent. They are small matters of detail, but I want to get everything right before I start.'

Tiger looked relieved. The raw animalism in Bond's face had been so different from the stoical, ironical face of the Bondo-san for whom he had come to have so much affection. He gave his great golden smile and said, 'But of course, my friend. And I am pleased with your worries and with the trouble you are taking to make sure of everything in advance. You will forgive me if I quote you one last Japanese proverb. It says, "A reasonable number of fleas is good for a dog. Otherwise the dog forgets he is a dog." '

'Good old Bashō!' said Bond.

13

KISSY SUZUKI

JAMES BOND went through the rest of the morning like an automaton. While he tried on his *ninja* equipment and watched each item being carefully packed into a floatable plastic container, his mind was totally occupied with the image of his enemy – this man Blofeld, the great gangster who had founded SPECTRE, the Special Executive for Counter-Intelligence, Terrorism, Revenge and Extortion, the man who was wanted by the police of all the NATO countries, the man who had murdered Tracy, Bond's wife for less than a day, a bare nine months ago. And, in those nine months, this evil genius had invented a new method of collecting death, as Tiger had put it. This cover as the Swiss Doctor Shatterhand, as a rich botanist, must have been one of the many he had wisely built up over the years. It would have been easy. A few gifts of rare plants to famous botanical gardens, the financing of a handful of expeditions, and all the while in the back of his mind the plan one day to retire and 'cultiver son jardin'. And what a garden! A garden that would be like a deadly fly-trap for human beings, a killing bottle for those who wanted to die. And of course, Japan, with the highest suicide statistics in the world, a country with an unquenchable thirst for the bizarre, the cruel and the terrible, would provide the perfect last refuge for him. Blofeld must have gone off his head, but with a monstrous, calculating madness – the madness of the genius he undoubtedly was. And the whole demoniac concept was on Blofeld's usual grand scale – the scale of a Caligula, of a Nero, of a Hitler, of any other great enemy of mankind. The speed of execution was breathtaking, the expenditure fabulous, the planning, down to the use of the Black Dragon Society, meticulous, and the cover as impeccable as the Piz Gloria Clinic which, less than a year before, Bond had helped to destroy utterly. And now the two enemies were lined up again, but this time David was spurred on to kill his Goliath not by duty but by blood feud! And with what weapons? Nothing but his bare hands, a two-inch pocket knife and a thin chain of steel. Well, similar weapons had served him before. Surprise would be the determining factor. Bond added a pair of black flippers to his equipment, a small supply of pemmican-like meat, benzedrine tablets, a plastic flask of water. Then he was ready.

They motored down the main street to where the police launch was waiting at the jetty and set off at a good twenty knots across the beautiful bay and round the headland into the Sea of Genkai. Tiger produced sandwiches and a flask of *sake* for each of them, and they ate their luncheon as the jagged green coast with its sandy beaches passed slowly by to port. Tiger pointed out a distant dot on the horizon. 'Kuro Island,' he said. 'Cheer up, Bondo-san! You seem preoccupied. Think of all those beautiful naked women you will soon be swimming with! And this Japanese Greta Garbo with whom you will be passing the nights!'

'And the sharks who will already be gathering at the news of my swim to the castle!'

'If they do not eat the Amas, why should they eat a bit of tough Englishman? Look at the two fish eagles circling! That is an excellent augury. One alone would have been less propitious. Four would have been disastrous, for with us four is the same as your thirteen – the worst number of all. But, Bondo-san, does it not amuse you to think of that foolish dragon dozing all unsuspecting in his castle while St George comes silently riding towards his lair across the waves? It would make the subject for a most entertaining Japanese print.'

'You've got a funny sense of humour, Tiger.'

'It is merely different from yours. Most of our funny stories involve death or disaster. I am not a "picture-daddy" – a professional story-teller – but I will tell you my favourite. It concerns the young girl who comes to the toll bridge. She tosses one sen, a very small piece of money, to the watchman, and walks on. The watchman calls after her, "Hey! You know that the toll for crossing the bridge is two sen." The girl answers, "But I do not intend to cross the bridge. I intend only to go halfway and then throw myself into the river."' Tiger laughed uproariously.

Bond smiled politely. 'I must save that one up for London. They'll split their sides over it.'

The small speck on the horizon grew larger and soon revealed itself as a horned island about five miles in circumference with steep cliffs and a small harbour facing north. On the mainland, Doctor Shatterhand's small peninsula reached out into the sea, and the fortress-like black wall soared up out of the breaking waves. Above it were the tops of trees, and, behind them, in the distance, the winged roof of the topmost storey of the castle broke the skyline. The formidable silhouette reminded Bond vaguely of photographs of Alcatraz taken from sea-level. He shivered slightly at the thought of the night's swim across the half-mile channel and of the black spider that would then scale those soaring fortifications. Ah well! He turned his attention back to Kuro Island.

It appeared to be made of black volcanic rock, but there was much green vegetation right up to the summit of a small peak on which there was some kind of a stone beacon. When they rounded the headland that formed one arm of the bay, a crowded little village and a jetty appeared. Out to sea, thirty or more rowing boats were scattered and there was the occasional glint of pink flesh in the sunlight. Naked children were playing among the big smooth black boulders that tumbled like bathing hippos along the shoreline, and there were green nets hung up to dry. It was a pretty scene, with the delicate remoteness, the fairyland quality, of small fishing communities all the world over. Bond took an immediate liking to the place, as if he was arriving at a destination that had been waiting for him and that would be friendly and welcoming.

A group of village elders, grave, gnarled old men with the serious expressions of simple people on important occasions, led by the Shinto priest, was on the jetty to welcome them. The priest was in ceremonial robes, a dark-red, three-quarter-length kimono with vast hanging sleeves, a turquoise skirt in broad pleats and the traditional shining black hat in the shape of a blunt cone. He was a man of simple dignity and considerable presence, middle-aged, with a round face and round spectacles and a pursed, judging mouth. His shrewd eye took them in one by one as they came ashore, but they rested longest on Bond. Superintendent Ando was greeted with friendship as well as respect. This was part of his parish, and he was the ultimate source of all fishing permits, reflected Bond ungraciously, but he had to admit that the deference of the bows was not exaggerated and that he was lucky in his ambassador. They proceeded up the cobbled path of the main

street to the priest's house, a modest, weather-beaten affair
of stone and carpentered driftwood. They entered and sat on
the spotless polished wood floor in an arc in front of the
priest, and the Superintendent made a long speech punctuated
by serious '*Hai*'s' and '*Ah, so desu ka*'s' from the priest, who
occasionally let his wise eyes rest thoughtfully on Bond. He
made a short speech in return, to which the Superintendent
and Tiger listened with deference. Tiger replied, and the
business of the meeting was over save for the inevitable
tea.

Bond asked Tiger how his presence and mission had been
explained. Tiger said that it would have been of no use lying
to the priest who was a shrewd man, so he had been told most
of the truth. The priest had expressed regret that such extreme
measures were contemplated, but he agreed that the castle
across the sea was a most evil place and its owner a man in
league with the devil. In the circumstances, he would give
the project his blessing and James Bond would be allowed to
stay on the island for the minimum time necessary to ac-
complish his mission.

The priest would invite the Suzuki family to accord him
an honourable welcome. Bond would be explained away to
the elders as a famous *gaijin* anthropologist who had come
to study the Ama way of life. Bond should therefore study
it, but the priest requested that Bond should behave in a
sincere manner. 'Which means,' explained Tiger with a
malicious grin, 'that you are not to go to bed with the girls.'

In the evening they walked back to the jetty. The sea was
a dark slate colour and mirror-calm. The little boats, bedecked
with coloured flags which meant that it had been an excep-
tional day's fishing, were winging their way back. The entire
population of Kuro, perhaps two hundred souls, was lined
up along the shore to greet the heroines of the day, the older
people holding carefully folded shawls and blankets to warm
up the girls on their way to their homes where, according to
Tiger, they would be given hot basin-baths to get back their
circulation and remove all traces of salt. It was now five o'clock.
They would be asleep by eight, said Tiger, and out again with

the dawn. Tiger was sympathetic. 'You will have to adjust your hours, Bondo-san. And your way of life. The Ama live very frugally, very cheaply, for their earnings are small – no more than the price of sparrows' tears, as we say. And for heaven's sake be very polite to the parents, particularly the father. As for Kissy . . .' He left the sentence hanging in the air.

Eager hands reached for each boat and, with happy shouts, pulled it up on the black pebbles. Big wooden tubs were lifted out and rushed up the beach to a kind of rickety market where, according to Tiger, the *awabi* were graded and priced. Meanwhile, the chattering, smiling girls waded in through the shallows and cast modestly appraising glances at the three mainland strangers on the jetty.

To Bond, they all seemed beautiful and gay in the soft evening light – the proud, rather coarse-nippled breasts, the gleaming, muscled buttocks, cleft by the black cord that held in place the frontal triangle of black cotton, the powerful thong round the waist with its string of oval lead weights, through which was stuck an angular steel pick, the white rag round the tumbled hair and, below, the laughing dark eyes and lips that were happy with the luck of the day. At that moment, it all seemed to Bond as the world, as life, should be, and he felt ashamed of his city-slicker appearance, let alone the black designs it concealed.

One girl, rather taller than the rest, seemed to pay no attention to the men on the jetty or to the police launch riding beside it. She was the centre of a crowd of laughing girls as she waded with a rather long, perhaps studied, stride over the shiny black pebbles and up the beach. She flung back a remark at her companions and they giggled, putting their hands up to their mouths. Then a wizened old woman held out a coarse brown blanket to her and she wrapped it round herself and the group dispersed.

The couple, the old woman and the young one, walked up the beach to the market. The young one talked excitedly. The old one paid attention and nodded. The priest was waiting for them. They bowed very low. He talked to them and they listened with humility, casting occasional glances towards the group on the jetty. The tall girl drew her blanket more closely round her. James Bond had guessed it already. Now he knew. This was Kissy Suzuki.

The three people, the splendidly attired priest, the walnut-faced old fisherwoman and the tall naked girl wrapped in her drab blanket came along the jetty, the girl hanging back. In a curious way they were a homogeneous trio, and the priest might have been the father. The women stopped and the priest came forward. He bowed to Bond and addressed him. Tiger translated: 'He says that the father and mother of Kissy Suzuki would be honoured to receive you in their humble abode for whose poverty they apologize. They regret that they are not accustomed to Western ways, but their daughter is proficient in English as a result of her work in America and will endeavour to convey your wishes to them. The priest asks if you can row a boat. The father, who previously rowed for his daughter, is stricken with rheumatism. It would be of great assistance to the family if you would deign to take his place.'

Bond bowed. He said, 'Please convey to his reverence that I am most grateful for his intercession on my behalf. I would be most honoured to have a place to lay my head in the home of Suzuki-san. My needs are very modest and I greatly enjoy the Japanese way of life. I would be most pleased to row the family boat or help the household in any other way.' He added, *sotto voce*, 'Tiger, I may need these people's help when the time comes. Particularly the girl's. How much can I tell her?'

Tiger said softly, 'Use your discretion. The priest knows, therefore the girl can know. She will not spread it abroad. And now come forward and let the priest introduce you. Don't forget that your name here is Taro, which means " first son ", Todoroki, which means "thunder". The priest is not interested in your real name. I have said that this is an approximation of your English name. It doesn't matter. Nobody will care. But you must try to assume some semblance of a Japanese personality for when you get to the other side. This name is on your identity card and on your miner's union card from the coal mines of Fukuoka. You need not bother with these things here for you are among friends. On the other side, if you are caught, you will show the card that says you are deaf and dumb. All right?'

Tiger talked to the priest and Bond was led forward to the two women. He bowed low to the mother, but he remembered not to bow too low as she was only a woman, and then he turned to the girl.

She laughed gaily. She didn't titter or giggle, she actually laughed. She said, 'You don't have to bow to me and I shall never bow to you.' She held out her hand. 'How do you do. My name is Kissy Suzuki.'

The hand was ice-cold. Bond said, 'My name is Taro Todoroki and I am sorry to have kept you here so long. You are cold and you ought to go and have your hot bath. It is very kind of your family to accept me as your guest, but I do not want to be an imposition. Are you sure it's all right?'

'Whatever the *kannushi-san,* the priest, says is all right. And I have been cold before. When you have finished with your distinguished friends, my mother and I will be happy to lead you to our house. I hope you are good at peeling potatoes.'

Bond was delighted. Thank God for a straightforward girl at last! No more bowing and hissing! He said, 'I took a degree in it. And I am strong and willing and I don't snore. What time do we take out the boat?'

'About five thirty. When the sun comes up. Perhaps you will bring me good luck. The *awabi* shells are not easy to find. We had a lucky day today and I earned about thirty dollars, but it is not always so.'

'I don't reckon in dollars. Let's say ten pounds.'

'Aren't Englishmen the same as Americans? Isn't the money the same?'

'Very alike, but totally different.'

'Is that so?'

'You mean "*Ah, so desu ka?*" '

The girl laughed. 'You have been well trained by the important man from Tokyo. Perhaps you will now say goodbye to him and we can go home. It is at the other end of the village.'

The priest, the Superintendent and Tiger had been talking

together, ostensibly paying no attention to Bond and the girl. The mother had been standing humbly, but with shrewd eyes, watching every expression on the two faces. Bond now bowed again to her and went back to the group of men.

Farewells were brief. Dusk was creeping up over the sea and the orange ball of the sun had already lost its brilliance in the evening haze. The engine of the police boat had been started up and its exhaust bubbled softly. Bond thanked the Superintendent and was wished good fortune in his honourable endeavours. Tiger looked serious. He took Bond's hand in both of his, an unusual gesture for a Japanese. He said, 'Bondo-san, I am certain you will succeed, so I will not wish you luck. Nor will I say *"sayōnara"*, farewell. I will simply say a quiet *"banzai!"* to you and give you this little *presento* in case the gods frown upon your venture and, through no fault of yours, things go wrong, very wrong.' He took out a little box and gave it to Bond.

The box rattled. Bond opened it. Inside was one long brownish pill. Bond laughed. He gave it back to Tiger and said, 'No thanks, Tiger. As Bashō said, or almost said, "You only live twice." If my second life comes up, I would rather look it in the face and not turn my back on it. But thanks, and thanks for everything. Those live lobsters were really delicious. I shall now look forward to eating plenty of sea-weed while I'm here. So long! See you in about a week.'

Tiger got down into the boat and the engine revved up. As the boat took the swell at the entrance to the harbour, Tiger raised a hand and brought it swiftly down with a chopping motion and then the boat was round the sea-wall and out of sight.

Bond turned away. The priest had gone. Kissy Suzuki said impatiently, 'Come along, Todoroki-san. The *kannushi-san* says I am to treat you as a comrade, as an equal. But give me one of those two little bags to carry. For the sake of the villagers who will be watching inquisitively, we will wear the Oriental face in public.'

And the tall man with the dark face, cropped hair and slanting eyebrows, the tall girl, and the old woman walked off along the shore with their angular Japanese shadows preceding them across the smooth black boulders.

14

ONE GOLDEN DAY

DAWN was a beautiful haze of gold and blue. Bond went outside and ate his bean curd and rice and drank his tea sitting on the spotless doorstep of the little cut-stone and timbered house, while indoors the family chattered like happy sparrows as the women went about their housework.

Bond had been allotted the room of honour, the small sitting-room with its *tatami* mats, scraps of furniture, house shrine and a cricket in a small cage 'to keep you company', as Kissy had explained. Here his *futon* had been spread on the ground and he had for the first time and with fair success tried sleeping with his head on the traditional wooden pillow. The evening before, the father, an emaciated greybeard with knotted joints and bright, squirrel eyes, had laughed with and at him as Kissy translated Bond's account of some of his adventures with Tiger, and there was from the first a complete absence of tension or self-consciousness. The priest had said that Bond should be treated as a member of the family and, although his appearance and some of his manners were strange, Kissy had apparently announced her qualified approval of him and the parents followed her lead. At nine o'clock, under the three-quarter moon, the father had beckoned to Bond and had hobbled out with him to the back of the house. He showed him the little shack with the hole in the ground and the neatly quartered pages of the *Asahi Shimbun* on a nail, and the last of Bond's private fears about life on the island was removed. His flickering candle showed the place to be as spotless as the house, and at least adequately salubrious. After the soft movements in the other two rooms had ceased, Bond had slept happily and like the dead.

Kissy came out of the house. She was wearing a kind of white cotton nightdress and a white cotton kerchief bound up the thick black waves of her hair. She wore her equipment, the weights and the heavy flat angular pick, over the white dress and only her arms and feet were bare. Bond may have shown his disappointment. She laughed, teasing him. 'This is ceremonial dress for diving in the presence of important strangers. The *kannushi-san* instructed me to wear it in your company. As a mark of respect, of course.'

'Kissy, I believe that is a fib. The truth of the matter is that you consider that your nakedness might arouse dishonourable thoughts in my impious Western mind. That is a most unworthy suspicion. However, I accept the delicacy of your respect of my susceptibilities. And now let's cut the cackle and get going. We'll beat the *awabi* record today. What should we aim at?'

'Fifty would be good. A hundred would be wonderful. But above all, you must row well and not let me drown. And you must be kind to David.'

'Who's David?' asked Bond, suddenly jealous at the thought that he would not be having this girl to himself.

'Wait and see.' She went back indoors and brought out the balsa wood tub and a great coil of fine quarter-inch rope. She handed the rope to Bond and hoisted the tub on her hip, leading the way along a small path away from the village. The path descended slowly to a small cove in which one rowing-boat, covered with dried reeds to protect it from the sun, was drawn high up on the flat black pebbles. Bond stripped off the reeds and laid them aside and hauled the simple, locally-made craft down to the sea. It was constructed of some heavy wood and lay low but stable in the deeply shelving, totally transparent water. He loaded in the rope and the wooden tub. Kissy had gone to the other side of the little bay and had undone a string from one of the rocks. She began winding it in slowly and at the same time uttering a low, cooing whistle. To Bond's astonishment, there was a flurry in the water of the bay and a big black cormorant shot like a bullet through the shallows and waddled up the beach to Kissy's feet, craning its neck up and down and hissing, apparently in anger. But Kissy bent down and stroked the creature on its plumed head and down the outstretched neck, at the same time talking to it gaily. She came towards the boat, winding up the long line, and the cormorant followed clumsily. It paid no attention to Bond, but jumped untidily over the side of the boat and scrambled on to the small thwart in the bows where it squatted majestically and proceeded to preen itself, running its long bill down and through its breast feathers and occasionally opening its wings to the full extent of their five-foot span and flapping them with gentle grace. Then, with a final shimmy through all its length, it settled down and gazed out to sea with its neck coiled backwards as if to strike and its turquoise eyes questing the horizon imperiously.

Kissy climbed into the boat and settled herself with her knees hunched decorously between Bond's outstretched legs, and Bond slid the heavy, narrow-bladed oars into their wooden rowlocks and began rowing at a powerful, even pace, more or less, under Kissy's direction, due north.

He had noticed that Kissy's line to the cormorant ended with a thin brass ring, perhaps two inches in diameter, round the base of the bird's neck. This would be one of the famous fishing cormorants of Japan. Bond asked her about it.

Kissy said, 'I found him as a baby three years ago. He had oil on his wings and I cleaned him and cared for him and had him ringed. The ring has had to be made larger as he grew up. Now, you see, he can swallow small fish, but the big ones he brings to the surface in his beak. He hands them over quite willingly and occasionally he gets a piece of a big one as a reward. He swims a lot by my side and keeps me company. It can be very lonely down there, particularly when the sea is dark. You will have to hold the end of the line and look after him when he comes to the surface. Today he will be hungry. He has not been out for three days because my father could not row the boat. I have been going out with friends. So it is lucky for him that you came to the island.'

'So this is David?'

'Yes. I named him after the only man I liked in Hollywood,

an Englishman as it happens. He was called David Niven. He is a famous actor and producer. You have heard of him?'

'Of course. I shall enjoy tossing him a scrap or two of fish in exchange for the pleasure he has given me in his other incarnation.'

The sweat began to pour down Bond's face and chest into his bathing pants. Kissy undid the kerchief round her hair and leant forward and mopped at him gently. Bond smiled into her almond eyes and had his first close-up of her snub nose and petalled mouth. She wore no make-up and did not need to, for she had that rosy-tinted skin on a golden background – the colours of a golden peach – that is quite common in Japan. Her hair, released from the kerchief, was black with dark-brown highlights. It was heavily waved, but with a soft fringe that ended an inch or so above the straight, fine eyebrows that showed no signs of having been plucked. Her teeth were even and showed no more prominently between the lips than with a European girl, so that she avoided the toothiness that is a weak point in the Japanese face. Her arms and legs were longer and less masculine than is usual with Japanese girls and, the day before, Bond had seen that her breasts and buttocks were firm and proud and that her stomach was almost flat – a beautiful figure, equal to that of any of the star chorus girls he had seen in the cabarets of Tokyo. But her hands and feet were rough and scarred with work, and her fingernails and toenails, although they were cut very short, were broken. Bond found this rather endearing. Ama means 'sea-girl' or 'sea-man', and Kissy wore the marks of competing with the creatures of the ocean with obvious indifference, and her skin, which might have suffered from constant contact with salt water, in fact glowed with a golden sheen of health and vitality. But it was the charm and directness of her eyes and smile as well as her complete naturalness – for instance, when she mopped at Bond's face and chest – that endeared her so utterly to Bond. At that moment, he thought there would be nothing more wonderful than to spend the rest of his life rowing her out towards the horizon during the day and coming back with her to the small, clean house in the dusk.

He shrugged the whimsy aside. Only another two days to the full moon and he would have to get back to reality, to the dark, dirty life he had chosen for himself. He put the prospect out of his mind. Today and the next day would be stolen days, days with only Kissy and the boat and the bird and the sea. He must just see to it that they were happy days and lucky ones for her and her harvest of seashells.

Kissy said, 'Not much longer. And you have rowed well.' She gestured to the right, to where the rest of the Ama fleet was spread out over the ocean. 'With us, it is first come first served with the sites we choose. Today we can get out as far as a shoal most of us know of, and we shall have it to ourselves. There the seaweed is thick on the rocks and that is what the *awabi* feed on. It is deep, about forty feet, but I can stay down for almost a minute, long enough to pick up two, three *awabi* if I can find them. That is just a matter of luck in feeling about with the hands among the seaweed, for you rarely see the shells. You only feel them and dislodge them with this,' she tapped her angular pick. 'After a while I shall have to rest. Then perhaps you would like to go down. Yes? They tell me you are a good swimmer and I have brought a pair of my father's goggles. These bulbs at the sides,' she showed him, 'have to be squeezed to equalize the pressure between the glasses and the eyes. You will perhaps not be able to stay down long to begin with. But you will learn quickly. How long will you be staying on Kuro?'

'Only two or three days, I'm afraid.'

'Oh, but that is sad. What will David and I do for a boat-man then?'

'Perhaps your father will get better.'

'That is so. I must take him to a cure place at one of the volcanoes on the mainland. Otherwise it will mean marrying one of the men on Kuro. That is not easy. The choice is not wide and, because I have a little money from my film work, and a little is a lot on Kuro, the man might want to marry me for the wrong reasons. That would be sad, and how is one to know?'

'Perhaps you will go back into films?'

Her expression became fierce. 'Never. I hated it. They were all disgusting to me in Hollywood. They thought that because I am a Japanese I am some sort of an animal and that my body is for everyone. Nobody treated me honourably except this Niven.' She shook her head to get rid of the memories. 'No. I will stay on Kuro for ever. The gods will solve my problems,' she smiled, 'like they have today.' She scanned the sea ahead. 'Another hundred yards.' She got up and balancing perfectly despite the swell, tied the end of the long rope round her waist and adjusted the goggles above her forehead. 'Now remember, keep the rope taut and when you feel one tug, pull me up quickly. It will be hard work for you, but I will massage your back when we get home this evening. I am very good at it. I have had enough practice with my father. Now!'

Bond shipped the oars gratefully. Behind him, David began shifting on his feet, craning his long neck and hissing impatiently. Kissy tied a short line to the wooden tub and put it over the side. She followed, slipping decorously into the water and clasping her white dress between her knees so that it did not flower out around her. At once David dived and disappeared without a ripple. The line, tied to Bond's thwart, began paying out fast. He picked up the coil of Kissy's rope and stood up, his joints cracking. Kissy pulled down her goggles and put her head underwater. In a moment she came up. She smiled. 'Yes, it looks fine down there.' She rested in the water and began making a soft cooing whistle through pursed lips – to fill her lungs to the uttermost, Bond assumed. Then, with a brief wave of the hand, she put down her head and arched her hips so that Bond had a brief sight of the black string cleaving her behind under the thin material. Suddenly, like a fleeting white wraith, she was gone, straight down, her feet twinkling behind her in a fast crawl to help the pull of the weights.

Bond paid out fast, keeping an anxious eye on his watch. David appeared below him, bearing a half-pound silvery fish crosswise in his beak. Damn the bird! This was no time to get mixed up with retrieving fish from the extremely sharp-looking beak. But, with a contemptuous glance, the cormorant tossed the fish into the floating tub and disappeared like a black bullet.

Fifty seconds! Bond started nervously when the tug came. He pulled in fast. The white wraith appeared far below in the crystal water, and, as she came up, Bond saw that her hands were tight against her sides to streamline her body. She broke surface beside the boat and held out two fat *awabi* to show him and then dropped them into the tub. She held on to the side of the boat to regain her breath and Bond gazed down at the wonderful breasts, taut beneath their thin covering. She smiled briefly up at him, began her cooing whistle, and then came the exciting arch of the back and she was gone again.

An hour went by. Bond got used to the routine and had time to watch the nearest of the fleet of other boats. They covered perhaps a mile of sea, and, from across the silent water, there came the recurrent eerie whistle – a soft, sea-bird sound – of the diving girls. The nearest boat rocked in the slow swell perhaps a hundred yards away, and Bond watched the young man at the rope and caught an occasional glimpse of a beautiful golden body, shiny as a seal, and heard the excited chattering of their voices. He hoped he would not disgrace himself when it came to his turn to dive. *Sake* and cigarettes! Not a good mixture to train on!

The pile of *awabi* was slowly growing in the tub and, amongst them, perhaps a dozen leaping fish. Occasionally Bond bent down and retrieved one from David. Once he dropped a slippery fish and the bird had to dive for it again. This time he received an even haughtier look of scorn from the turquoise eyes.

Then Kissy came up, her stint done, and climbed, not so decorously this time, into the boat, and tore off her kerchief and goggles and sat panting quietly in the stern. Finally she looked up and laughed happily. 'That is twenty-one. Very good. Now take my weights and pick and see for yourself what it is like down there. But I will pull you up anyway in thirty seconds. Give me your watch. And please do not lose my *tegane*, my pick, or our day's fishing will be over.'

Bond's first dive was a clumsy affair. He went down too slowly and barely had time to survey the grassy plain, scattered with black rocks and clumps of *Posidonia*, the common sea-weed of all the oceans, when he felt himself being hauled up. He had to admit to himself that his lungs were in terrible shape, but he had spied one promising rock thick with weed and on his next dive he got straight to it and clung, searching among the roots with his right hand. He felt the smooth oval of a shell, but before he could get the pick to it he was being pulled up again. But he got the shell on his third try, and Kissy laughed with pleasure as he dropped it into the tub. He managed to keep the diving up for about half an hour, but then his lungs began to ache and his body to feel the cold of the October sea and he came up for the last time simultaneously with David, who shot past him like a beautiful gleaming black fish with green highlights and, as a mark of approval, pecked gently at his hair as Bond deposited his fifth shell in the tub.

Kissy was pleased with him. She had a rough brown kimono in the boat and she rubbed him down with it as he sat with bowed head and heaving chest. Then, while he rested, she hauled the wooden tub inboard and emptied its contents into the bottom of the boat. She produced a knife and cut one of the fish down the middle and fed the two halves to David who was riding expectantly beside the boat. He swallowed the pieces in two great gulps and set to preening his feathers contentedly.

Later they stopped for a lunch of rice with a few small bits of fish in it and dried seaweed which tasted of salty spinach. And then, after a short rest in the bottom of the boat, the work went on until four o'clock, when a small chill breeze came from nowhere and got between them and the warmth of the sun and it was time to make the long row home. Kissy climbed for the last time into the boat and gave several soft tugs at David's line. He surfaced some distance from the boat and, as if this was a well-worn routine, rose into the air and circled round them again and again before making a low dive and skiing in to the side of the boat on his webbed feet. He flapped his way over the side and went to his perch, where he stood with wings magnificently outstretched to dry and waited in this lordly stance for his boatman to take him back home to his cove.

Kissy changed with extreme propriety into her brown kimono and dried herself inside it. She announced that their haul was sixty-five *awabi*, which was quite wonderful. Of these Bond was responsible for ten, which was a very honourable first catch. Ridiculously pleased with himself, Bond took a vague bearing on the island which, because of the drifting of the boat, was now only a speck on the horizon, and gradually worked himself into the slow unlaboured sweep of a Scottish gillie.

His hands were sore, his back ached as if he had been thrashed with a wooden truncheon, and his shoulders were beginning to sting with sunburn, but he comforted himself with the reflection that he was only doing what he would have had to do anyway – get into training for the swim and the climb and what would come afterwards, and he rewarded himself from time to time with a smile into Kissy's eyes. They never left him and the low sun shone into them and turned the soft brown to gold. And the speck became a lump, and the lump an island and at last they were home.

15

THE SIX GUARDIANS

THE next day was as golden as the first and the haul of *awabi* went up to sixty-eight, largely thanks to Bond's improved diving.

The evening before, Kissy had come back from selling her shells at the market and had found Bond writhing on the floor of his room with cramps in his stomach muscles and her mother clucking helplessly over him. She had shooed her mother away, spread the soft *futon* on the floor beside him and had pulled off his bathing pants and rolled him on to the *futon* face downwards. Then she had stood upright on his back and had walked softly up and down his spine from his buttocks to his neck, and the ache had slowly gone. She told him to lie still and brought him warm milk. Then she led him into the tiny bathhouse and poured hot and then tepid water over him from an *awabi* tub until all the salt was out of his skin and hair. She dried him softly, rubbed warm milk into his sunburn and his chafed hands, and led him back to his room, telling him with gentle sternness to go to sleep and to call her if he awoke in the night and needed anything. She blew out his candle and left him, and he went out, to the night-song of the cricket in its cage, like a light.

In the morning, nothing remained of his aches except the soreness of the hands, and Kissy gave him the rare treat of an egg beaten up in his rice and bean curd and he apologized for his bad manners of the night before. She said, 'Todoroki-san, you have the spirit of ten *samurai*, but you have the body of only one. I should have known that I had asked too much of that single body. It was the pleasure of the day. It made me forget everything else. So it is I who apologize, and today we will not go so far. Instead, we will keep close to the cliffs of the island and see what we can find. I will do the rowing, for it is a small distance, but you will be able to do more diving because the place that I know of, which I haven't visited for many weeks, is inshore and the water is, at the most, twenty feet deep.'

And so it had been, and Bond had worn a shirt to protect him from the sun and his tally of shells had gone up to twenty-one, and the solitary shadow of the day had been the clear view he had had of the black fortress across the straits and the chunky yellow-and-black warning balloon that flew the column of black ideograms above it.

During one of their rests, Bond casually asked Kissy what she knew of the castle, and he was surprised by the way her face darkened. 'Todoroki-san, we do not usually talk about that place. It is almost a forbidden subject on Kuro. It is as if hell had suddenly opened its mouth half a mile away across the sea from our home. And my people, the Ama, are like what I have read about your gipsies. We are very superstitious. And we believe the devil himself has come to live over there.' She didn't look at the fortress, but gestured with her head. 'Even the *kannushi-san* does not deny our fears, and our elders say that the *gaijins* have always been bad for Japan and that this one is the incarnation of all the evil in the West. And there is already a legend that has grown up on the island. It is that our six *Jizo* Guardians will send a man from across the sea to slay this "King of Death", as we call him.'

'Who are these Guardians?'

'*Jizo* is the god who protects children. He is, I think, a Buddhist god. On the other side of the island, on the foreshore, there are five statues. The sixth has been mostly washed away. They are rather frightening to see. They squat there in a line. They have rough bodies of stone and round stones for heads and they wear white shirts that are changed by the people every month. They were put there centuries ago by our ancestors. They sit on the line of low tide, and as the tide comes up it covers them completely and they keep watch under the surface of the sea and protect us, the Ama, because we are known as "The Children of the Sea". At the beginning of every June, when the sea is warm after the winter and the diving begins, every person on the island forms into a procession and we go to the Six Guardians and sing to them to make them happy and favourable towards us.'

'And this story of the man from Kuro. Where did it come from?'

'Who knows? It could have come from the sea or the air and thus into the minds of the people. Where do stories like that come from? It is widely believed.'

'*Ah, so desu ka!*' said Bond, and they both laughed and got on with the work.

On the third day, when Bond was as usual eating his breakfast on the doorstep, Kissy came to the doorway and said softly, 'Come inside, Todoroki-san.' Mystified, he went in and she shut the door behind him.

She said in a low voice, 'I have just heard from a messenger from the *kannushi-san* that there were people here yesterday in a boat from the mainland. They brought *presentos* – cigarettes and sweets. They were asking about the visit of the police boat. They said it came with three visitors and left with only two. They wanted to know what had happened to the third visitor. They said they were guards from the castle and it was their duty to prevent trespassers. The elders accepted the *presentos*, but they showed *shiran-kao*, which is "the face of him who knows nothing", and referred the men to the *kannushi-san* who said that the third visitor was in charge of fishing licences. He had felt sick on the way to the island and had perhaps lain down in the boat on the way back. Then he dismissed the men and sent a boy to the top of the High Place to see where the boat went, and the boy reported that it went to the bay beside the castle and was put back into the boathouse that is there. The *kannushi-san* thought that you should know these things.' She looked at him piteously. 'Todoroki-san, I have a feeling of much friendship for you. I feel that there are secret things between you and the *kannushi-san*, and that they concern the castle. I think you should tell me enough to put me out of my unhappiness.'

Bond smiled. He went up to her and took her face in both his hands and kissed her on the lips. He said, 'You are very beautiful and kind, Kissy. Today we will not take the boat out because I must have some rest. Lead me up to the High Place from which I can take a good look at this castle and I will tell you what I can. I was going to anyway, for I shall need your help. Afterwards, I would like to visit the Six Guardians. They interest me – as an anthropologist.'

Kissy collected their usual lunch in a small basket, put on her brown kimono and rope-soled shoes and they set off along a small footpath that zigzagged up the peak behind the crouching grey cluster of the village. The time of the camellia was almost past, but here there were occasional bushes of wild camellias in red and white, and there was a profusion of these round a small grove of dwarf maples, some of which already wore their flaming autumn colours. The grove was directly above Kissy's house. She led him in and showed him the little Shinto shrine behind a rough stone *torii*. She said, 'Behind the shrine there is a fine cave, but the people of Kuro are afraid of it as it is full of ghosts. But I explored it once and if there are ghosts there they are friendly ones.' She clapped her hands before the shrine, bent her head for a moment, and clapped them again. Then they went on up the path to the top of the thousand-foot peak. A brace of gorgeous copper pheasants with golden tails fled squawking over the brow and down to a patch of bushes on the southern cliff as they approached. Bond told Kissy to stay out of sight while he went and stood behind the tall cairn of stones on the summit and gazed circumspectly round it and across the straits.

He could see over the high fortress wall and across the park to the towering black-and-gold donjon of the castle. It was ten o'clock. There were figures in blue peasant dress with high boots and long staves moving busily about the grounds. They occasionally seemed to prod into the bushes with their staves. They wore black *maskos* over their mouths. It crossed Bond's mind that they might be doing the morning rounds looking for overnight prey. What did they do when they found some half-blinded creature, or a pile of clothes beside one of the fumaroles whose little clouds of steam rose here and there in the park? Take them to the Doctor? And, in the case of the living, what happened then? And when he, Bond, got up that wall tonight, where was he going to hide from the guards? Well, sufficient unto the day! At least the straits were calm and it was cloudless weather. It looked as if he would get there all right. Bond turned away and went back to Kissy and sat with her on the sparse turf. He gazed across the harbour to where the Ama fleet lay sprawled across the middle distance.

He said, 'Kissy, tonight I have to swim to the castle and climb the wall and get inside.'

She nodded. 'I know this. And then you are going to kill this man and perhaps his wife. You are the man who we believe was to come to Kuro from across the sea and do these things.' She continued to gaze out to sea. She said dully, 'But why have you been chosen? Why should it not be another, a Japanese?'

'These people are *gaijins*. I am a *gaijin*. It will cause less trouble for the State if the whole matter is presented as being trouble between foreigners.'

'Yes, I see. And has the *kannushi-san* given his approval?'

'Yes.'

'And if . . . And after. Will you come back and be my boat-
man again?'

'For a time. But then I must go back to England.'

'No. I believe that you will stay for a long time on Kuro.'

'Why do you believe that?'

'Because I prayed for it at the shrine. And I have never
asked for such a big thing before. I am sure it will be granted.'
She paused. 'And I shall be swimming with you tonight.' She
held up a hand. 'You will need company in the dark and I
know the currents. You would not get there without me.'

Bond took the small dry paw in his. He looked at the
childish, broken nails. His voice was harsh. He said, 'No. This
is man's work.'

She looked at him. The brown eyes were calm and serious.
She said, and she used his first name, 'Taro-san, your other
name may mean thunder, but I am not frightened of thunder.
I have made up my mind. And I shall come back every night,
at midnight exactly, and wait among the rocks at the bottom
of the wall. I shall wait for one hour in case you need my
help in coming home. These people may harm you. Women
are much stronger in the water than men. That is why it is the
Ama girls who dive and not the Ama men. I know the waters
round Kuro as a peasant knows the fields round his farm, and
I have as little fear of them. Do not be stiff-necked in this
matter. In any case, I shall hardly sleep until you come back.
To feel that I am close to you for a time and that you may need
me will give me some peace. Say yes, Taro-san.'

'Oh, all right, Kissy,' said Bond gruffly. 'I was only going
to ask you to row me to a starting point down there somewhere.' He gestured to the left across the straits. 'But if you
insist on being an extra target for the sharks . . .'

'The sharks never trouble us. The Six Guardians look
after that. We never come to any harm. Years ago, one of the
Amas caught her rope in a rock underwater, and the people
have talked of the accident ever since. The sharks just think
we are big fish like themselves.' She laughed happily. 'Now
it is all settled and we can have something to eat and then I

will take you down to see the Guardians. The tide will be low by then and they will want to inspect you.'

They followed another little path from the summit. It went over the shoulder of the peak and down to a small protected bay to the east of the village. The tide was far out and they could wade over the flat black pebbles and rocks and round the corner of the promontory. Here, on a stretch of flat stony beach, five people squatted on a square foundation of large rocks and gazed out towards the horizon. Except that they weren't people. They were, as Kissy had described, stone pedestal bodies with large round boulders cemented to their tops. But rough white shirts were roped round them, and they looked terrifyingly human as they sat in immobile judgement and guardianship over the waters and what went on beneath them. Of the sixth, only the body remained. His head must have been destroyed by a storm.

They walked round in front of the five and looked up at the smooth blank faces and Bond, for the first time in his life, had a sensation of deep awe. So much belief, so much authority seemed to have been invested by the builders in these primitive, faceless idols, guardians of the blithe, naked Ama girls, that Bond had a ridiculous urge to kneel and ask for their blessing as the Crusaders had once done before their God. He brushed the impulse aside, but he did bow his head and briefly ask for good fortune to accompany his enterprise. And then he stood back and watched with a pull at his heart-strings while Kissy, her beautiful face strained and pleading, clapped to attract their attention and then made a long and impassioned speech in which his name recurred. At the end, when she again clapped her hands, did the round boulder-heads briefly nod? Of course not! But, when Bond took Kissy's hand and they walked away, she said happily, 'It is all right, Todoroki-san. You saw them nod their heads?'

'No,' said Bond firmly, 'I did not.'

They crept round the eastern shore of Kuro and pulled the boat up into a deep cleft in the black rocks. It was just after

eleven o'clock and the giant moon rode high and fast through
wisps of mackerel cloud. They talked softly, although they
were out of sight of the fortress and half a mile away from it.
Kissy took off her brown kimono and folded it neatly and put
it in the boat. Her body glowed in the moonlight. The black
triangle between her legs beckoned, and the black string round
her waist that held the piece of material was an invitation to un-
tie it. She giggled provocatively. 'Stop looking at my Black
Cat!'

'Why is it called that?'

'Guess!'

Bond carefully pulled on his *ninja* suit of black cotton. It
was comfortable enough and would give warmth in the
water. He left the head-shroud hanging down his back and
pushed the goggles that belonged to Kissy's father up his
forehead. The small floating pack he was to tow behind him
rode jauntily in the waters of the creek, and he tied its string
firmly to his right wrist so that he would always know it was
there.

He smiled at Kissy and nodded.

She came up to him and threw her arms round his neck and
kissed him full on the lips.

Before he could respond, she had pulled down her goggles
and had dived into the quiet, mercury sea.

16

THE LOVESOME SPOT

KISSY'S crawl was steady and relaxed and Bond had no difficulty in following the twinkling feet and the twin white
mounds of her behind, divided excitingly by the black cord.
But he was glad he had donned flippers because the tug of
his floating container against the wrist was an irritating brake
and, for the first half of the swim, they were heading diagon-
ally against the easterly current through the straits. But then

Kissy slightly changed her direction and now they could paddle lazily in towards the soaring wall that soon became their whole horizon.

There were a few tumbled rocks at its base, but Kissy stayed in the water, clinging to a clump of seaweed, in case the moon might betray her gleaming body to a sentry or a chance patrol, though Bond guessed that the guards kept clear of the grounds during the night so that the suicides would have free entry. Bond pulled himself up on the rocks and unzipped the container and extracted the packet of iron pitons. Then he climbed up a few feet so that he could stow his flippers away in a crack between the granite blocks above high water mark, and he was ready to go. He blew a kiss to the girl. She replied with the sideways wave of the hand that is the Japanese sign of farewell and then was off across the sea again, a luminous white torpedo that merged quickly into the path of the moon.

Bond put her out of his thoughts. He was getting chilled in his soaking black camouflage and it was time to get moving. He examined the fitting of the giant stone blocks and found that the cracks between them were spacious, as in the case of Tiger's training castle, and would probably provide adequate toe-holds. Then he pulled down his black cowl, and, towing the black container behind him, began his climb.

It took him twenty minutes to cover the two hundred feet of the slightly inclined wall, but he only had to use his pitons twice when he came to cracks that were too narrow to give a hold to his aching toes. And then he was at one of the gun-ports, and he slithered quietly across its six feet of flat masonry and cautiously looked over the edge into the park. As he had expected, there were stone steps down from the gun-port, and he crept down these into the dark shadows at its base and stood up against the inside of the wall panting quietly. He waited for his breath to calm down and then slipped back his cowl and listened. Not a wisp of wind stirred in the trees, but from somewhere came the sound of softly running water and, in the background, a regular, glutinous burping and bubbling. The fumaroles! Bond, a black shadow among the rest, edged along the wall to his right. His first task was to find a hideout, a base camp where he could bivouac in emergency and where he could leave his container. He reconnoitred various groves and clumps of bushes, but they were all damnably well-kept and the undergrowth had been meticulously cleared from their roots. And many of them exuded a sickly-sweet, poisonous night-smell. Then, up against the wall, he came upon a lean-to shed, its rickety door ajar. He listened and then inched the door open. As he had expected, there was a shadowy jumble of gardeners' tools, wheelbarrows and the like, and the musty smell of such places. Moving carefully, and helped by shafts of moonlight through the wide cracks in the planked walls, he got to the back of the hut where there was an untidy mound of used sacking. He reflected for a moment, and decided that though this place would be often visited, it had great promise. He untied the cord of the container from his wrist and proceeded methodically to move some of the sacks forward so as to provide a nest for himself behind them. When it was finished, and final touches of artistic disarray added, he parked his container behind the barrier and crept out again into the park to continue what he planned should be a first quick survey of the whole property.

Bond kept close to the boundary wall, flitting like a bat across the open spaces between clumps of bushes and trees. Although his hands were covered with the black material of the *ninja* suit, he avoided contact with the vegetation, which emitted a continually changing variety of strong odours and scents amongst which he recognized, as a result of ancient adventures in the Caribbean, only the sugary perfume of dogwood. He came to the lake, a wide silent shimmer of silver from which rose the thin cloud of steam he remembered from the aerial photograph. As he stood and watched it, a large leaf from one of the surrounding trees came wafting down and settled on the surface near him. At once a quick, purposeful ripple swept down on the leaf from the surrounding water and immediately subsided. There were some kind of fish in the lake and they would be carnivores. Only carnivores would be excited like that at the hint of a prey. Beyond the lake, Bond came on the first of the fumaroles, a sulphurous, bubbling pool of mud that constantly shuddered and spouted up little fountains. From yards away, Bond could feel its heat. Jets of stinking steam puffed out and disappeared, wraithlike, towards the sky. And now the jagged silhouette of the castle, with its winged turrets, showed above the tree-line, and Bond crept forward with the added caution, alert for the moment when he would come upon the treacherous gravel that surrounded it. Suddenly, through a belt of trees, he was facing it. He stopped in the shelter of the trees, his heart hammering under his ribcage.

Close to, the soaring black-and-gold pile reared monstrously over him, and the diminishing curved roofs of the storeys were like vast bat-wings against the stars. It was even bigger than Bond had imagined, and the supporting wall of black granite blocks more formidable. He reflected on the seemingly impossible problem of entry. Behind would be the main entrance, the lowish wall and the open countryside. But didn't castles always have an alternative entrance low down for a rearward escape? Bond stole cautiously forward, laying his feet flat down so that the gravel barely stirred. The many eyes of the castle, glittering white in the moonlight, watched his approach with the indifference of total power. At any moment, he had expected the white shaft of a searchlight or the yellow-and-blue flutter of gunfire. But he reached the base of the wall without incident and followed it along to the left, remembering from ancient schooling that most castles had an exit at moat level beneath the drawbridge.

And so it was with the castle of Doctor Shatterhand – a small nail-studded door, arched and weather-beaten. Its hinges and lock were cracked and rusty, but a new padlock and chain had been stapled into the woodwork and the stone frame. No moonlight filtered down to this corner of what must once have been a moat, but was now grassed over. Bond felt carefully with his fingers. Yes! The chain and lock would yield to the file and jemmy in his conjurer's pockets. Would there be bolts on the inner side? Probably not, or the padlock would not have been thought necessary. Bond softly retraced his steps across the gravel, stepping meticulously in his previous footmarks. That door would be his target for tomorrow!

Now, keeping right-handed, but still following the boundary wall, he crept off again on his survey. Once, something slithered away from his approaching feet and disappeared with a heavy rustle into the fallen leaves under a tree. What snakes were there that really went for a man? The king-cobra, black mamba, the saw-scaled viper, the rattlesnake and the fer de lance. What others? The remainder were inclined to make off if disturbed. Were snakes day or night hunters? Bond didn't know. Among so many hazards, there weren't even the odds of Russian Roulette. When all the chambers of the pistol were loaded, there was not even a one in six chance to bank on.

Bond was now on the castle side of the lake. He heard a noise and edged behind a tree. The distant crashing in the shrubbery sounded like a wounded animal, but then, down the path, came staggering a man, or what had once been a man. The brilliant moonlight showed a head swollen to the size of a football, and only small slits remained where the eyes and mouth had been. The man moaned softly as he zig-zagged along, and Bond could see that his hands were up to his puffed face and that he was trying to prise apart the swollen skin round his eyes so that he could see out. Every now and then he stopped and let out one word in an agonizing howl to the moon. It was not a howl of fear or of pain, but of dreadful supplication. Suddenly he stopped. He seemed to see the lake for the first time. With a terrible cry, and holding out his arms as if to meet a loved one, he made a quick run to the edge and threw himself in. At once there came the swirl of movement Bond had noticed before, but this time it involved a great area of water and there was a wild boiling of the surface round the vaguely threshing body. A mass of small fish were struggling to get at the man, particularly at the naked hands and face, and their six-inch bodies glittered and flashed in the moonlight. Once the man raised his head and let out a single, terrible scream and Bond saw that his face was encrusted with pendent fish as if with silvery locks of hair. Then his head fell back into the lake and he rolled over and over as if trying to rid himself of his attackers. But slowly the black stain spread and spread around him and finally, perhaps because his jugular had been pierced, he lay still, face downwards in the water, and his head jigged slightly with the ceaseless momentum of the attack.

James Bond wiped the cold sweat off his face. Piranha! The South American fresh-water killer whose massive jaws and flat, razor-sharp teeth can strip a horse down to the bones in under an hour! And this man had been one of the suicides who had heard of this terrible death! He had come searching for the lake and had got his face poisoned by some pretty shrub. The Herr Doktor had certainly provided a feast for his victims. Unending dishes for their delectation! A true banquet of death!

James Bond shuddered and went on his way. All right, Blofeld, he thought, that's one more notch on the sword that is already on its way to your neck. Brave words! Bond hugged the wall and kept going. Gunmetal was showing in the east.

But the Garden of Death hadn't quite finished the display of its wares.

All over the park, a slight smell of sulphur hung in the air, and many times Bond had had to detour round steaming cracks in the ground and the quaking mud of fumaroles, identified by a warning circle of white-painted stones. The Doctor was most careful lest anyone should fall into one of these liquid furnaces by mistake! But now Bond came to one the size of a circular tennis-court, and here there was a rough shrine in the grotto at the back of it and, dainty touch, a vase with flowers in it – chrysanthemums, because it was now officially winter and therefore the chrysanthemum season. They were arranged with some sprigs of dwarf maple, in a pattern which no doubt spelled out some fragrant message to the initiates of Japanese flower arrangement. And opposite the grotto, behind which Bond in his ghostly black uniform crouched in concealment, a Japanese gentleman stood in rapt contemplation of the bursting mud-boils that were erupting genteelly in the simmering soup of the pool. James Bond thought 'gentleman' because the man was dressed in the top hat, frock-coat, striped trousers, stiff collar and spats of a high government official – or of the father of the bride. And the gentleman held a carefully rolled umbrella between his clasped hands, and his head was bowed over its crook as if in penance. He was speaking, in a soft compulsive babble, like someone in a highly ritualistic church, but he made no gestures and just stood, humbly, quietly, either confessing or asking one of the gods for something.

Bond stood against a tree, black in the blackness. He felt he should intervene in what he knew to be the man's purpose. But how to do so knowing no Japanese, having nothing but his 'deaf and dumb' card to show? And it was vital that he should remain a 'ghost' in the garden, not get involved in some daft argument with a man he didn't know, about some ancient sin he could never understand. So Bond stood, while the trees threw long black arms across the scene, and waited, with a cold, closed, stone face, for death to walk on stage.

The man stopped talking. He raised his head and gazed up at the moon. He politely lifted his shining top hat. Then he replaced it, tucked his umbrella under one arm and sharply clapped his hands. Then walking, as if to a business appointment, calmly, purposefully, he took the few steps to the edge of the bubbling fumarole, stepped carefully over the warning stones and went on walking. He sank slowly in the glutinous grey slime and not a sound escaped his lips until, as the tremendous heat reached his groin, he uttered one rasping 'Arrghh!' and the gold in his teeth showed as his head arched back in the rictus of death. Then he was gone and only the top hat remained, tossing on a small fountain of mud that spat intermittently into the air. Then the hat slowly crumpled with the heat and disappeared, and a great belch was uttered from the belly of the fumarole and a horrible stench of cooking meat overcame the pervading stink of sulphur and reached Bond's nostrils.

Bond controlled his rising gorge. Honourable salary-man had gone to honourable ancestors – his unknown sin expiated as his calcined bones sank slowly down into the stomach of the world. And one more statistic would be run up on Blofeld's abacus of death. Why didn't the Japanese Air Force come and bomb this place to eternity, set the castle and the poison garden ablaze with napalm? How could this man continue to have protection from a bunch of botanists and scientists? And now here was he, Bond, alone in this hell to try and do the job with almost no weapon but his bare hands. It was hopeless! He was scarcely being given a chance in a million. Tiger and his Prime Minister were certainly exacting their pound of flesh in exchange for their precious MAGIC 44 – one hundred and eighty-two pounds of it to be exact!

Cursing his fate, cursing Tiger, cursing the whole of Japan, Bond went on his way, while a small voice whispered in his ear, 'But don't you want to kill Blofeld? Don't you want to avenge Tracy? Isn't this a God-given chance? You have done well tonight. You have penetrated his defences and spied out the land. You have even found a way into his castle and probably up to his bedroom. Kill him in his sleep to-morrow! And kill her too, while you're about it! And then back into Kissy's arms and, in a week or two, back over the Pole to London and to the applause of your Chief. Come on! Somewhere in Japan, a Japanese is committing suicide every thirty minutes all through the year. Don't be squeamish because you've just seen a couple of numbers ticked off on a sheet in the Ministry of Health, a couple of points added to a graph. Snap out of it! Get on with the job.'

And Bond listened to the whisper and went on round the last mile of wall and back to the gardeners' hut.

He took a last look round before going in. He could see a neck of the lake about twenty yards away. It was now gun-metal in the approaching dawn. Some big insects were flitting and darting through the softly rising steam. They were pink dragonflies. Pink ones. Dancing and skimming. But of course! The *haiku* of Tiger's dying agent! That was the last night-marish touch to this obscenity of a place. Bond went into the hut, picked his way carefully between the machines and wheel-barrows, pulled some sacks over himself and fell into a shallow sleep full of ghosts and demons and screams.

17

SOMETHING EVIL COMES THIS WAY

THE dreamed screams had merged into real ones when, four hours later, Bond awoke. There was silence in the hut. Bond got cautiously to his knees and put his eye to a wide crack in the rickety planking. A screaming man, from his ragged blue cotton uniform a Japanese peasant, was running across his line of vision along the edge of the lake. Four guards were after him, laughing and calling as if it were a game of hide-and-seek. They were carrying long staves, and now one of them paused and hurled his stave accurately after the man so that it caught in his legs and brought him crashing to the ground. He scrambled to his knees and held supplicating hands out towards his pursuers. Still laughing, they gathered round him, stocky men in high rubber boots, their faces made terrifying by black *maskos* over their mouths, black leather nose-pieces and the same ugly black leather soup-plate hats as the agent on the train had worn. They poked at the man with the ends of their staves, at the same time shouting harshly at him in voices that jeered. Then, as if at an order, they bent down and, each man seizing a leg or an arm, picked him off the ground, swung him once or twice and tossed him out into the lake. The ghastly ripple surged forward and the man, now screaming again, beat at his face with his hands and floundered as if trying to make for the shore, but the screams rapidly became weaker and finally ceased as the head went down and the red stain spread wider and wider.

Doubled up with laughter, the guards on the bank watched the show. Now, satisfied that the fun was over, they turned away and walked towards the hut, and Bond could see the tears of their pleasure glistening on their cheeks.

He got back under cover and heard their boisterous voices and laughter only yards away as they came into the hut and pulled out their rakes and barrows and dispersed to their jobs, and for some time Bond could hear them calling to each other across the park. Then, from the direction of the castle, came the deep tolling of a bell, and the men fell silent. Bond glanced at the cheap Japanese wristwatch Tiger had provided. It was nine o'clock. Was this the beginning of the official working day? Probably. The Japanese usually get to their work half an hour early and leave half an hour late in order to gain face with their employer and show keenness and gratitude for their jobs. Later, Bond guessed, there would be an hour's luncheon break. Work would probably cease at six. So it would only be from six thirty on that he would have the grounds to himself. Meanwhile, he must listen and watch and find out more about the guards' routines, of which he had presumably witnessed the first – the smelling out and final dispatch of suicides who had changed their minds or turned faint-hearted during the night. Bond softly unzipped his container and took a bite at one of his three slabs of pemmican and a short draught from his water-bottle. God, for a cigarette!

An hour later, Bond heard a brief shuffling of feet on the gravel path on the other side of the lake. He looked through the slit. The four guards had lined up and were standing rigidly to attention. Bond's heart beat a little faster. This would be for some form of inspection. Might Blofeld be doing his rounds, getting his reports of the night's bag?

Bond strained his eyes to the right, towards the castle, but his view was obstructed by an expanse of white oleanders, that innocent shrub with its attractive clusters of blossom that is used as a deadly fish poison in many parts of the tropics. Dear, pretty bush! Bond thought. I must remember to keep clear of you tonight.

And then, following the path on the other side of the lake, two strolling figures came into his line of vision and Bond clenched his fists with the thrill of seeing his prey.

Blofeld, in his gleaming chain armour and grotesquely

spiked and winged helmet of steel, its visor closed, was something out of Wagner, or, because of the oriental style of his armour, a Japanese *Kabuki* play. His armoured right hand rested easily on a long naked *samurai* sword while his left was hooked into the arm of his companion, a stumpy woman with the body and stride of a wardress. Her face was totally obscured by a hideous bee-keeper's hat of dark-green straw with a heavy pendent black veil reaching down over her shoulders. But there could be no doubt! Bond had seen that dumpy silhouette, now clothed in a plastic rainproof above tall rubber boots, too often in his dreams. That was her! That was Irma Bunt!

Bond held his breath. If they came round the lake to his side, one tremendous shove and the armoured man would be floundering in the water! But could the piranhas get at him through chinks in the armour? Unlikely! And how would he, Bond, get away? No, that wouldn't be the answer.

The two figures had almost reached the line of four men, and at this moment the guards dropped to their knees in unison and bowed their foreheads down to the ground. Then they quickly jumped up and stood again at attention.

Blofeld raised his visor and addressed one of the men, who answered with deference. Bond noticed for the first time that this particular guard wore a belt round his waist with a holstered automatic. Bond couldn't hear the language they were speaking. It was impossible that Blofeld had learned Japanese. English or German? Probably the latter as a result of some wartime liaison job. The man laughed and pointed towards the lake, where a collapsed balloon of blue clothing was jigging softly with the activities of the horde of feasting piranhas within it. Blofeld nodded his approval and the men again went down on their knees. Blofeld raised a hand in brief acknowledgement, lowered his visor and the couple moved regally on.

Bond watched carefully to see if the file of guards, when they got to their feet, registered any private expressions of scorn or hilarity once The Master's back was turned. But there was no hint of disrespect. The men broke ranks and hurried off about their tasks with disciplined seriousness, and Bond was reminded of Dikko Henderson's illustration of the automatic, ant-like subservience to discipline and authority of the Japanese that had resulted in one of the great crimes of the century. If only dear Dikko were here now. What a tremendous boost his fists and his surging zest would add to this lunatic operation!

The crime had concerned, said Dikko, a modest suburban branch of the Imperial Bank. It had been a normal day of business, when a man wearing an official-looking armband had presented himself to the manager of the bank. He was from the Ministry of Health. An outbreak of typhus was feared and he would be obliged if the manager would line up his staff in the courtyard so that he could administer the official antidote. The manager bowed and complied, and, after everything had been locked up, the fourteen staff assembled and listened carefully to the short lecture on health delivered by the man with the armband. Then everyone had bowed in acknowledgement of the wisdom of the Ministry of Health, and the official had bent to his small suitcase and produced fifteen glasses into which he measured medicine from a bottle. He handed a glass to each person and advised them to swallow the mixture at one gulp as otherwise it might damage their teeth. 'Now,' he had said, according to Dikko's version. 'All together! One. Two. Three!' And down went the honourable medicine and down fell the honourable local manager and staff of the Imperial Bank of Japan. The medicine had been neat cyanide.

The 'Ministry of Health official' had removed the keys from the trouser-pocket of the prone manager, had loaded up his car with two hundred and fifty million yen, and had driven cheerfully from the scene of what was to become known as the 'Teigin case' after the suburb in which it took place.

And here, Bond reflected, was the same total obedience to authority, but in this case the tacit approval and sympathy of the Black Dragon philosophy was operating. Blofeld told them to do such things as he had witnessed a couple of hours before. He was invested with power from certain departments of State. He had dressed for the part. His orders were obeyed. And there was honourable job to be done. Honourable job which resulted in much publicity in the newspapers. And this was a powerful *gaijin* who had powerful squeeze in high places and 'a wide face'. And if people wanted to kill themselves, why worry? If the Castle of Death, with perhaps an occasional extra push, was not available, they would choose the railways or the trams. Here was a public service. Almost a sub-department of the Ministry of Health! So long as their *maskos* and nose-pieces protected them from the poisons in the garden, the main thing was to do their jobs conscientiously and perhaps, one day, they would get a Minister of Self-Destruction appointed in the Diet! Then the great days of the Black Dragon *Kōan* would come again to save the Country of the Rising Sun from the creeping paralysis of *demokorasu*!

And now the two strolling figures were coming back into Bond's line of vision, but this time from the left. They had rounded the end of the lake and were on their way back, perhaps to visit other groups of guards and get their reports. Tiger had said there were at least twenty guards and that the property covered five hundred acres. Five working parties of four guards each? Blofeld's visor was up and he was talking to the woman. They were now only twenty yards away. They stopped at the edge of the lake and contemplated, with relaxed curiosity, the still turbulent mass of fish round the floating doll of blue cloth. They were talking German. Bond strained his ears.

Blofeld said, 'The piranhas and the volcanic mud are useful housekeepers. They keep the place tidy.'

'The sea and the sharks are also useful.'

'But often the sharks do not complete the job. That spy we put through the Question Room. He was almost intact when his body was found down the coast. The lake would have been a better place for him. We don't want that policeman from Fukuoka coming here too often. He may have means of learning from the peasants how many people are crossing the wall. That will be many more, nearly double the number the ambulance comes for. If our figures go on increasing at this rate, there is going to be trouble. I see from the cuttings Kono translates for me that there are already mutterings in the papers about a public inquiry.'

'And what shall we do then, lieber Ernst?'

'We shall obtain massive compensation and move on. The same pattern can be repeated in other countries. Everywhere there are people who want to kill themselves. We may have to vary the attractions of the opportunities we offer them. Other people have not the profound love of horror and violence of the Japanese. A really beautiful waterfall. A handy bridge. A vertiginous drop. These might be alternatives. Brazil, or somewhere else in South America, might provide such a site.'

'But the figures would be much smaller.'

'It is the concept that matters, liebe Irma. It is very difficult to invent something that is entirely new in the history of the world. I have done that. If my bridge, my waterfall, yields a crop of only perhaps ten people a year, it is simply a matter of statistics. The basic idea will be kept alive.'

'That is so. You are indeed a genius, lieber Ernst. You have already established this place as a shrine to death for evermore. People read about such fantasies in the works of Poe, Lautréamont, de Sade, but no one has ever created such a fantasy in real life. It is as if one of the great fairy tales has come to life. A sort of Disneyland of Death. But of course,' she hastened to add, 'on an altogether grander, more poetic scale.'

'In due course I shall write the whole story down. Then perhaps the world will acknowledge the type of man who has been living among them. A man not only unhonoured and unsung, but a man' – Blofeld's voice rose almost to a scream – 'whom they hunt down and wish to shoot like a mad dog. A man who has to use all his wiles just to stay alive! Why, if I had not covered my tracks so well, there would be spies on their way even now to kill us both or to hand us over for official murder under their stupid laws! Ah well, liebe Irma,' the voice was more rational, quieter, 'we live in a world of fools in which true greatness is a sin. Come! It is time to review the other detachments.'

They turned away and were about to continue along the lake when Blofeld suddenly stopped and pointed like a dog directly at Bond. 'That hut among the bushes. The door is open! I have told the men a thousand times to keep such places locked. It is a perfect refuge for a spy or a fugitive. I will make sure.'

Bond shivered. He huddled down, dragging sacks from the top of his barrier to give extra protection. The clanking steps approached, entered the hut. Bond could feel the man, only yards away, could feel his questing eyes and nostrils. There came a clang of metal and the wall of sacks shook at great thrusts from Blofeld's sword. Then the sword slashed down again and again and Bond winced and bit his lip as a hammer-blow crashed across the centre of his back. But then Blofeld seemed to be satisfied and the iron steps clanged away. Bond let out his breath in a quiet hiss. He heard Blofeld's voice say, 'There is nothing, but remind me to reprimand Kono on our rounds tomorrow. The place must be cleared out and a proper lock fitted.' Then the sound of the steps vanished in the direction of the oleander clump, and Bond gave a groan and felt his back. But, though many of the sacks above him had been sliced through, his protection had been just deep enough and the skin across his spine wasn't broken.

Bond got to his knees and rearranged the hideout, massaging his aching back as he did so. Then he spat the dust from the sacking out of his mouth, took a swallow from the water-bottle, assured himself through his slit that there was no movement outside and lay down and let his mind wander back over every word that Blofeld had uttered.

Of course the man was mad. A year earlier, the usual quiet tones that Bond remembered so well would never have cracked into that lunatic, Hitler scream. And the coolness, the supreme confidence that had always lain behind his planning? Much of that seemed to have seeped away, perhaps, Bond hoped, partly because of the two great failures he, Bond, had done much to bring about in two of Blofeld's most grandiose conspiracies. But one thing was clear – the hideout was blown. Tonight would have to be the night. Ah, well!

Once again Bond ran over the hazy outline of his plan. If he could gain access to the castle, he felt pretty confident of finding a means to kill Blofeld. But he was also fairly certain that he himself would die in the process. *Dulce et decorum est* . . . and all that jazz! But then he thought of Kissy, and he wasn't so sure about not fearing for himself. She had brought a sweetness back into his life that he thought had gone for ever.

Bond dropped off into an uneasy, watchful sleep that was once again peopled by things and creatures out of nightmare-land.

18

OUBLIETTE

AT SIX O'CLOCK in the evening, the deep bell tolled briefly from the castle and dusk came like the slow drawing of a violet blind over the day. Crickets began to zing in a loud chorus and geckos chuckled in the shrubbery. The pink dragonflies disappeared and large horned toads appeared in quantities from their mud holes on the edge of the lake and, so far as Bond could see through his spy-hole, seemed to be catching gnats attracted by the shining pools of their eyes. Then the four guards reappeared, and there came the fragrant smell of a bonfire they had presumably lit to consume the refuse they had collected during the day. They went to the edge of the lake and raked in the tattered scraps of blue clothing and, amidst delighted laughter, emptied long bones out of the fragments into the water. One of them ran off with the rags, presumably to add them to the bonfire, and Bond got under cover as the others pushed their wheel-barrows up the slope and stowed them away in the hut. They stood chattering happily in the dusk until the fourth arrived and then, without noticing the slashed and disarrayed sacks in the shadows, they filed off in the direction of the castle.

After an interval, Bond got up and stretched and shook the dust out of his hair and clothes. His back still ached, but his overwhelming sensation was the desperate urge for a cigarette. All right. It might be his last. He sat down and drank a little water and munched a large wedge of the highly-flavoured pemmican, then took another swig at the water-bottle. He took out his single packet of Shinsei and lit up, holding the cigarette between cupped hands and quickly blowing out the match. He dragged the smoke deep down into his lungs. It was bliss! Another drag and the prospect of the night seemed less daunting. It was surely going to be all right! He thought briefly of Kissy who would now be eating her bean curd and fish and preparing the night's swim in her mind. A few hours more and she would be near him. But what would have happened in those few hours? Bond smoked the cigarette until it burned his fingers, then crushed out the stub and pushed the dead fragments down through a crack in the floor. It was seven thirty and already some of the insect noises of sundown had ceased. Bond went meticulously about his preparations.

At nine o'clock he left the hideout. Again the moon blazed down and there was total silence except for the distant burping and bubbling of the fumaroles and the occasional sinister chuckle of a gecko from the shrubbery. He took the same route as the night before, came through the same belt of trees and stood looking up at the great bat-winged donjon that towered up to the sky. He noticed for the first time that the warning balloon with its advertisement of danger was tethered to a pole on the corner of the balustrade surrounding what appeared to be the main floor – the third, or centre one of the five. Here, from several windows, yellow light shone faintly, and Bond guessed that this would be his target area. He let out a deep sigh and strode quietly off across the gravel and came without incident to the tiny entrance under the wooden bridge.

The black *ninja* suit was as full of concealed pockets as a conjurer's tail coat. Bond took out a pencil flashlight and a small steel file and set to work on a link of the chain. Occasionally he paused to spit into the deepening groove to lessen

the rasp of metal on metal, but then there came the final crack
of parting steel and, using the file as a lever, he bent the link
open and quietly removed the padlock and chain from its
stanchions. He pressed lightly and the door gave inwards.
He took out his flashlight and pushed farther, probing the
darkness ahead with his thin beam. It was as well he did so.
On the stone floor where his first step past the open door
would have taken him, lay a yawning man-trap, its rusty iron
jaws, perhaps a yard across, waiting for him to step on the
thin covering of straw that partially concealed it. Bond winced
as, in his imagination, he heard the iron clang as the
saw-teeth bit into his leg below the knee. There would be
other such booby-traps – he must keep every sense on the
alert!

Bond closed the door softly behind him, stepped round
the trap and swept the beam of his torch ahead and around
him. Nothing but velvety blackness. He was in some vast
underground cellar where no doubt the food supplies for a
small army had once been stored. A shadow swept across
the thin beam of light and another and another, and there was a
shrill squeaking from all around him. Bond didn't mind bats
or believe the Victorian myth that they got caught in your
hair. Their radar was too good. He crept slowly forward,
watching only the rough stone flags ahead of him. He passed
one or two bulky arched pillars, and now the great cellar
seemed to narrow because he could just see walls to right and
left of him and above him an arched, cobwebby roof. Yes,
here were the stone steps leading upwards! He climbed them
softly and counted twenty of them before he came to the
entrance, a wide double door with no lock on his side. He
pushed gently and could feel and hear the resistance of a
rickety-sounding lock. He took out a heavy jemmy and probed.
Its sharp jaws notched round some sort of a cross-bolt, and
Bond levered hard sideways until there came the tearing sound
of old metal and the tinkle of nails or screws on stone. He
pushed softly on the crack and, with a hideously loud report,
the rest of the lock came away and half the door swung open
with a screech of old hinges. Beyond was more darkness.

Bond stepped through and listened, his torch doused. But he was still deep in the bowels of the castle and there was no sound. He switched on again. More stone stairs leading up to a modern door of polished timber. He went up them and carefully turned the metal door handle. No lock this time! He softly pushed the door open and found himself in a long stone corridor that sloped on upwards. At the end was yet another modern door, and beneath it showed a thin strip of light!

Bond walked noiselessly up the incline and then held his breath and put his ear to the keyhole. Dead silence! He grasped the handle and inched the door open and then, satisfied, went through and closed the door behind him, leaving it on the latch. He was in the main hall of the castle. The big entrance door was on his left, and a well-used strip of red carpet stretched away from it and across the fifty feet of hall into the shadows that were not reached by the single large oil lamp over the entrance. The hall was not embellished in any way, save for the strip of carpet, and its roof was a maze of longitudinal and cross beams interspersed with latticed bamboo over the same rough plaster-work as covered the walls. There was still the same castle-smell of cold stone.

Bond kept away from the carpet and hugged the shadows of the walls. He guessed that he was now on the main floor and that somewhere straight ahead was his quarry. He was well inside the citadel. So far so good!

The next door, obviously the entrance to one of the public rooms, had a simple latch to it. Bond bent and put his eye to the keyhole. Another dimly lit interior. No sound! He eased up the latch, inched the door ajar, and then open, and went through. It was a second vast chamber, but this time one of baronial splendour – the main reception room, Bond guessed, where Blofeld would receive visitors. Between tall red curtains, edged with gold, fine set-pieces of armour and weapons hung on the white plaster walls, and there was much heavy antique furniture arranged in conventional groupings on a vast central carpet in royal blue. The rest of the floor was of highly polished boards, which reflected back the lights from two great oil lanterns that hung from the high, timbered roof, similar to that of the entrance hall, but here with the main beams decorated in a zigzag motif of dark red. Bond, looking for places of concealment, chose the widely spaced curtains and, slipping softly from one refuge to the next, reached the small door at the end of the chamber that would, he guessed, lead to the private apartments.

He bent down to listen, but immediately leaped for cover behind the nearest curtains. Steps were approaching! Bond undid the thin chain from around his waist, wrapped it round his left fist and took the jemmy in his right hand and waited, his eyes glued to a chink in the dusty-smelling material.

The small door opened halfway to show the back of one of the guards. He wore a black belt with a holster. Would this be Kono, the man who translated for Blofeld? He had probably had some job with the Germans during the war – in the Kempeitai, perhaps. What was he doing? He appeared to be fiddling with some piece of apparatus behind the door. A light switch? No, there was no electric light. Apparently satisfied, the man backed out, bowed deeply to the interior and closed the door. He wore no *masko* and Bond caught a brief glimpse of a surly, slit-eyed brownish face as he passed Bond's place of concealment and walked on across the reception chamber. Bond heard the click of the far door and then there was silence. He waited a good five minutes before gently shifting the curtain so that he could see down the room. He was alone.

And now for the last lap!

Bond kept his weapons in his hands and crept back to the door. This time no sound came from behind it. But the guard had bowed. Oh well! Probably out of respect for the aura of The Master. Bond quietly but firmly thrust the door open and leaped through, ready for the attacking sprint.

A totally empty, totally featureless length of passageway yawned at his dramatics. It stretched perhaps twenty feet in front of him. It was dimly lit by a central oil lamp and its floor was of the usual highly polished boards. A 'nightingale floor'? No. The guard's footsteps had uttered no warning creaks. But from behind the facing door at the end came the sound of music. It was Wagner, the 'Ride of the Valkyries', being played at medium pitch. Thank you, Blofeld! thought Bond. Most helpful cover! And he crept softly forward down the centre of the passage.

When it came, there was absolutely no warning. One step across the exact halfway point of the flooring and, like a seesaw, the whole twenty feet of boards swivelled noiselessly on some central axis and Bond, arms and legs flailing and hands scrabbling desperately for a grip, found himself hurtling down into a black void. The guard! The fiddling about behind the door! He had been adjusting the lever that set the trap, the traditional oubliette of ancient castles! And Bond had forgotten! As his body plunged off the end of the inclined platform into space, an alarm bell, triggered by the mechanism of the trap, brayed hysterically. Bond had a fractional impression of the platform, relieved of his weight, swinging back into position above him, then he crashed shatteringly into unconsciousness.

Bond swam reluctantly up through the dark tunnel towards the blinding pinpoint of light. Why wouldn't someone stop hitting him? What had he done to deserve it? He had got two *awabis*. He could feel them in his hands, sharp-edged and rough. That was as much as Kissy could expect of him. 'Kissy,' he mumbled, 'stop it! Stop it, Kissy!'

The pinpoint of light expanded, became an expanse of straw-covered floor on which he was crouching while the open hand crashed sideways into his face. Piff! Paff! With each slap the splitting pain in his head exploded into a thousand separate pain fragments. Bond saw the edge of the boat above him and desperately raised himself to grasp at it. He held up the *awabis* to show that he had done his duty. He opened his hands to drop them into the tub. Consciousness flooded back and he saw the two handfuls of straw dribble to the ground. But the blows had stopped. And now he could see, indistinctly, through a mist of pain. That brown face! Those slit eyes! Kono, the guard. And someone else was holding a torch for him. Then it all came back. No *awabis*! No Kissy! Something dreadful had happened! Everything had gone wrong! *Shimata!* I have made a mistake! Tiger! The clue clicked and total realization swept through Bond's mind. Careful, now. You're deaf and dumb. You're a Japanese miner from Fukuoka. Get the record straight. To hell with the pain in your head. Nothing's broken. Play it cool. Bond put his hands down to his sides. He realized for the first time that he was naked save for the brief vee of the black cotton *ninja* underpants. He bowed deeply and straightened himself. Kono, his hand at his open holster, fired furious Japanese at him. Bond licked at the blood that was trickling down his face and looked blank, stupid. Kono took out his small automatic, gestured. Bond bowed again, got to his feet, and, with a brief glance round the straw-strewn oubliette into which he had fallen, followed the unseen guard with the torch out of the cell.

There were stairs and a corridor and a door. Kono stepped forward and knocked.

And then Bond was standing in the middle of a small, pleasant, library-type room and the second guard was laying out on the floor Bond's *ninja* suit and the appallingly incriminating contents of his pockets. Blofeld, dressed in a magnificent black silk kimono across which a golden dragon sprawled, stood leaning against the mantelpiece beneath which a Japanese brazier smouldered. It was him all right. The bland, high forehead, the pursed purple wound of a mouth, now shadowed by a heavy grey-black moustache that drooped at the corners, on its way, perhaps, to achieving mandarin proportions, the mane of white hair he had grown for the part of Monsieur le Comte de Bleuville, the black bullet-holes of the eyes. And beside him, completing the picture of a homely couple at ease after dinner, sat Irma Bunt, in the full regalia of a high-class Japanese lady, the petit point of a single chrysanthemum lying in her lap waiting for those pudgy hands to take it up when the cause of this unseemly disturbance had been ascertained. The puffy, square face, the tight bun of mousy hair, the thin wardress mouth, the light-brown, almost yellow eyes! By God, thought Bond dully, here they are! Within easy reach! They would both be dead by now but for his single criminal error. Might there still be some way of turning the tables? If only the pain in his head would stop throbbing!

Blofeld's tall sword stood against the wall. He picked it up and strode out into the room. He stood over the pile of Bond's possessions and picked them over with the tip of the sword. He hooked up the black suit. He said in German, 'And what is this, Kono?'

The head guard replied in the same language. His voice was uneasy and his eye-slits swivelled with a certain respect towards Bond and away again. 'It is a *ninja* suit, Herr Doktor. These are people who practise the secret arts of *ninjutsu*. Their secrets are very ancient and I know little of them. They are the art of moving by stealth, of being invisible, of killing without weapons. These people used to be much feared in Japan. I was not aware that they still existed. This man has undoubtedly been sent to assassinate you, my lord. But for the magic of the passage, he might well have succeeded.'

'And who is he?' Blofeld looked keenly at Bond. 'He is tall for a Japanese.'

'The men from the mines are often tall men, my lord. He carries a paper saying that he is deaf and dumb. And other papers, which appear to be in order, stating that he is a miner from Fukuoka. I do not believe this. His hands have some broken nails, but they are not the hands of a miner.'

'I do not believe it either. But we shall soon find out.' Blofeld turned to the woman. 'What do you think, my dear? You have a good nose for such problems – the instincts of a woman.'

Irma Bunt rose and came and stood beside him. She looked piercingly at Bond and then walked slowly round him, keeping her distance. When she came to the left profile she said softly, with awe, '*Du lieber Gott!*' She went back to Blofeld. She said in a hoarse whisper, still staring, almost with horror, at Bond, 'It cannot be! But it is! The scar down the right cheek! The profile! And the eyebrows have been shaved to give that upward tilt!' She turned to Blofeld. She said decisively, 'This is the English agent. This is the man Bond, James Bond, the man whose wife you killed. The man who went under the

name of Sir Hilary Bray.' She added fiercely, 'I swear it!
You have got to believe me, lieber Ernst!'

Blofeld's eyes had narrowed. 'I see a certain resemblance.
But how has he got here? How has he found me? Who sent
him?'

'The Japanese *Geheimdienst*. They will certainly have
relations with the British Secret Service.'

'I cannot believe it! If that was so, they would have come
with warrants to arrest me. There are too many unknown
factors in this business. We must proceed with great circum-
spection and extract the whole truth from this man. We must
at once find out if he is deaf and dumb. That is the first step.
The Question Room should settle that. But first of all he
must be softened up.' He turned to Kono. 'Tell Kazama to
get to work.'

19

THE QUESTION ROOM

THERE were now ten guards in the room. They stood lined
up against the wall behind Kono. They were all armed with
their long staves. Kono fired an order at one of them. The
man left his stave in an angle of the wall and came forward.
He was a great, box-like man with a totally bald, shining head
like a ripe fruit and hands like hams. He took up his position
in front of Bond, his legs straddled for balance and his lips
drawn back in a snarling smile of broken black teeth. Then
he swung his right hand sideways at Bond's head and slapped
him with tremendous force exactly on the bruise of Bond's
fall. Bond's head exploded with fire. Then the left hand came
at him and Bond rocked sideways. Through a mist of blood
he could see Blofeld and his woman. Blofeld was merely
interested, as a scientist, but the woman's lips were parted
and wet.

Bond took ten blows and knew that he must act while he

still had the purpose and the strength. The straddled legs offered the perfect target. So long as the man had not practised the *Sumo* trick! Through a haze, Bond took aim and, as another giant blow was on its way, kicked upwards with every ounce of force left to him. His foot slammed home. The man gave an animal scream and crashed to the ground, clasping himself and rolling from side to side in agony. The guards made a concerted rush forward, their staves lifted, and Kono had his gun out. Bond leaped for the protection of a tall chair, picked it up and hurled it at the snarling pack of guards. One of the legs caught a man in the teeth and there was the sound of splintering bone. The man went down clutching his face.

'Halt!' It was the Hitlerian scream Bond had heard before. The men stood stock still and lowered their staves. 'Kono. Remove those men.' Blofeld pointed down at the two casualties. 'And punish Kazama for his incompetence. Get new teeth for the other one. And enough of this. The man will not speak with ordinary methods. If he can hear, he will not withstand the pressure of the Question Room. Take him there. The rest of the guards can wait in the audience chamber. *Also! Marsch!*'

Kono fired off orders to which the guards reacted at the double. Then Kono gestured to Bond with his gun, opened a small doorway beside the bookcase and pointed down a narrow stone passage. Now what? Bond licked the blood from the corners of his mouth. He was near the end of his tether. Pressure? He couldn't stand much more of it. And what was this Question Room? He mentally shrugged. There might still be a chance to get at Blofeld's throat. If only he could take that one with him! He went ahead down the passage, was deaf to the order from Kono to open the rough door at the end, had it opened for him by the guard while the pistol pressed into his spine, and walked forward into a bizarre room of roughly hewn stone that was very hot and stank disgustingly of sulphur.

Blofeld and the woman entered, the door was closed and they took their places in two wooden armchairs beneath an oil lamp and a large kitchen clock whose only unusual feature was that, at each quarter, the figures were underlined in red. The hands stood at just after eleven and now, with a loud iron tick, the minute hand dropped one span. Kono gestured for Bond to advance the twelve paces to the far end of the room where there was a raised stone pedestal-seat with arms. It dripped with drying grey mud and there was the same volcanic filth on the floor all round it. Above the stone seat, in the ceiling, there was a wide circular opening through which Bond could see a patch of dark sky and stars. Kono's rubber boots squelched after him and Bond was gestured to sit down on the stone throne. In the centre of the seat there was a large round hole. Bond did as he was told, his skin flinching at the hot sticky surface of the mud. He rested his forearms wearily on the stone arms of the throne and waited, his belly crawling with the knowledge of what this was all about.

Blofeld spoke from the other end of the room. He spoke in English. He said, in a loud voice that boomed round the naked walls, 'Commander Bond, or number 007 in the British Secret Service if you prefer it, this is the Question Room, a device of my invention that has the almost inevitable effect of making silent people talk. As you know, this property is highly volcanic. You are now sitting directly above a geyser that throws mud, at a heat of around one thousand degrees Centigrade, a distance of approximately one hundred feet into the air. Your body is now at an elevation of approximately fifty feet directly above its source. I had the whimsical notion to canalize this geyser up a stone funnel above which you now sit. This is what is known as a periodic geyser. This particular example is regulated to erupt volcanically on exactly each fifteenth minute in every hour.' Blofeld looked behind him and turned back. 'You will therefore observe that you have exactly eleven minutes before the next eruption. If you cannot hear me, or the translation that will follow, if you are a deaf and dumb Japanese as you maintain, you will not move from that chair and, at the fifteenth minute past eleven, you will suffer a most dreadful death by the incineration of your lower body. If, on the other hand, you leave the seat before the death moment, you will have demonstrated that you can hear and understand and you will then be put to further tortures which will inevitably make you answer my questions. These questions will seek to confirm your identity, how you come to be here, who sent you and with what purpose, and how many people are involved in the conspiracy. You understand? You would not prefer to give up this play-acting? Very well. On the off chance that your papers are perhaps partially correct, my chief guard will now briefly explain the purpose of this room in the Japanese language.' He turned to the guard. 'Kono *sag' ihm auf japanisch den Zweck dieses Zimmers.'*

Kono had taken up his position by the door. He now harangued Bond in sharp Japanese sentences. Bond paid no attention. He concentrated on regaining his strength. He sat relaxed and gazed nonchalantly round the room. He had remembered the final 'hell' at Beppu and he was looking for something. Ah yes! There it was! A small wooden box in the corner to the right of his throne. There was no keyhole to it. Inside that box would undoubtedly be the regulating valve for the geyser. Could that bit of knowledge be put to some use? Bond tucked it away and racked his tired brain for some kind of a plan. If only the agonizing pulse in his head would stop. He rested his elbows on his knees and gently lowered his bruised face into his hands. At least that guard would now be in even worse agony than he!

Kono stopped talking. The clock uttered a deep iron tick. It ticked nine times more. Bond looked up at the black-and-white clockwork face. It said 11.14. A deep, angry grumble sounded from deep down beneath him. It was followed by a hard buffet of very hot breath. Bond got to his feet and walked slowly away from the stinking stone vent until he reached the area of the floor that was not wet with mud. Then he turned and watched. The grumble had become a far-away roar. The roar became a deep howl that swelled up into the room like an express train coming out of a tunnel. Then there was a mighty explosion and a solid jet of grey mud shot like a gleaming grey piston out of the hole Bond had just left and exactly penetrated the wide aperture in the ceiling.

The jet continued, absolutely solid, for perhaps half a second, and searing heat filled the room so that Bond had to wipe the sweat from his forehead. Then the grey pillar collapsed back into the hole and mud pattered on to the roof of the place and splashed down into the room in great steaming gobbets. A deep bubbling and burping came up the pipe and the room steamed. The stench of sulphur was sickening. In the total silence that followed, the tick of the clock to 11.16 was as loud as a gong-stroke.

Bond turned and faced the couple under the clock. He said cheerfully, 'Well, Blofeld, you mad bastard. I'll admit that your effects man down below knows his stuff. Now bring on the twelve she-devils and if they're all as beautiful as Fräulein Bunt, we'll get Noël Coward to put it to music and have it on Broadway by Christmas. How about it?'

Blofeld turned to Irma Bunt. 'My dear girl, you were right! It is indeed the same *Britischer*. Remind me to buy you another string of the excellent Mr Mikimoto's grey pearls. And now let us be finished with this man once and for all. It is beyond our bedtime.'

'Yes indeed, lieber Ernst. But first he must speak.'

'Of course, Irmchen. But that can be quickly done. We have already broken his first reserves. The second line of defence will be routine. Come!'

Back up the stone passage! Back into the library! Irma Bunt back to her petit point, Blofeld back to his stance by the mantelpiece, his hand resting lightly on the boss of his great sword. It was just as if they had returned after taking part in some gracious after-dinner entertainment: a game of billiards, a look at the stamp albums, a dull quarter of an hour with the home movies. Bond decided: to hell with the Fukuoka miner! There was a writing-desk next to the bookshelves. He pulled out its chair and sat down. There were cigarettes and matches. He lit up and sat back, inhaling luxuriously. Might as well make oneself comfortable before one went for The Big Sleep! He tapped his ash on to the carpet and crossed one knee over the other.

Blofeld pointed to the pile of Bond's possessions on the

floor. 'Kono, take those away. I will examine them later. And you can wait with the guards in the outer hall. Prepare the blowlamp and the electrical machine for further examination in case it should be necessary.' He turned to Bond. 'And now – talk and you will receive an honourable and quick death by the sword. Have no misgivings. I am expert with it and it is razor-sharp. If you do not talk, you will die slowly and horribly and you will talk just the same. You know from your profession that this is so. There is a degree of prolonged suffering that no human can withstand. Well?'

Bond said easily, 'Blofeld, you were never stupid. Many people in London and Tokyo know of my presence here tonight. At this moment, you might argue your way out of a capital charge. You have a lot of money and you could engage the best lawyers. But, if you kill me, you will certainly die.'

'Mister Bond, you are not telling the truth. I know the ways of officialdom as well as you do. Therefore I dismiss your story in its entirety and without hesitation. If my presence here was officially known, a small army of policemen would have been sent to arrest me. And they would have been accompanied by a senior member of the CIA on whose WANTED list I certainly feature. This is an American sphere of influence. You might have been allowed to interview me subsequent to my arrest, but an Englishman would not have featured in the initial police action.'

'Who said this was police action? When, in England, I heard rumours about this place, I thought the whole project smelled of you. I obtained permission to come and have a look. But my whereabouts is known and retribution will result if I do not return.'

'That does not follow, Mister Bond. There will be no trace of your ever having seen me, no trace of your entry into the property. I happen to have certain information that fits in with your presence here. One of my agents recently reported that the Head of the Japanese Secret Service, the *Kōan-Chōsa-Kyōku*, a certain Tanaka, came down in this direction accompanied by a foreigner dressed as a Japanese. I now see that your appearance tallies with my agent's description.'

'Where is this man? I would like to question him.'

'He is not available.'

'Very convenient.'

A red fire began to burn deep in the black pools of Blofeld's eyes. 'You forget that it is not I who am being interrogated, Mister Bond. It is you. Now, I happen to know all about this Tanaka. He is a totally ruthless man, and I will hazard a guess that fits the facts and that is made almost into a certitude by your crude evasions. This man Tanaka has already lost one senior agent whom he sent down here to investigate me. You were available, on some business concerned with your profession, perhaps, and, for a consideration, or in exchange for a favour, you agreed to come here and kill me, thus tidying up a situation which is causing some embarrassment to the Japanese Government. I do not know or care when you learned that Doctor Guntram Shatterhand was in fact Ernst Stavro Blofeld. You have your private reasons for wanting to kill me, and I have absolutely no doubt that you kept your knowledge to yourself and passed it on to no one for fear that the official action I have described would take the place of your private plans for revenge.' Blofeld paused. He said softly, 'I have one of the greatest brains in the world, Mister Bond. Have you anything to say in reply? As the Americans say, "It had better be good." '

Bond took another cigarette and lit it. He said composedly, 'I stick to the truth, Blofeld. If anything happens to me, you, and probably the woman as an accessory, will be dead by Christmas.'

'All right, Mister Bond. But I am so sure of my facts that I am now going to kill you with my own hands and dispose of your body without more ado. On reflection, I would rather do it myself than have it done slowly by the guards. You have been a thorn in my flesh for too long. The account I have to settle with you is a personal one. Have you ever heard the Japanese expression "*kirisute gomen*"?'

Bond groaned. 'Spare me the Lafcadio Hearn, Blofeld!'

'It dates from the time of the *samurai*. It means literally "killing and going away". If a low person hindered the *samurai's* passage along the road or failed to show him proper respect, the *samurai* was within his rights to lop off the man's head. I regard myself as a latter-day *samurai*. My fine sword has not yet been blooded. Yours will be an admirable head to cut its teeth on.' He turned to Irma Bunt. 'You agree, mein Liebchen?'

The square wardress face looked up from its petit point. 'But of course, lieber Ernst. What you decide is always correct. But be careful. This animal is dangerous.'

'You forget, mein Liebchen. Since last January he has ceased to be an animal. By a simple stroke of surgery on the woman he loved, I reduced him to human dimensions.'

The dominant, horrific figure stood away from the mantelpiece and took up his sword.

'Let me show you.'

20

BLOOD AND THUNDER

BOND dropped his lighted cigarette and left it to smoulder on the carpet. His whole body tensed. He said, 'I suppose you know you're both mad as hatters.'

'So was Frederick the Great, so was Nietzsche, so was Van Gogh. We are in good, in illustrious company, Mister Bond. On the other hand, what are you? You are a common thug, a blunt instrument wielded by dolts in high places. Having done what you are told to do, out of some mistaken idea of duty or patriotism, you satisfy your brutish instincts with alcohol, nicotine and sex while waiting to be dispatched on the next misbegotten foray. Twice before, your Chief has sent you to do battle with me, Mister Bond, and, by a combination of luck and brute force, you were successful in destroying two projects of my genius. You and your government would categorize these projects as crimes against humanity, and various authorities still seek to bring me to book for them. But try and summon such wits as you possess, Mister Bond, and see them in a realistic light and in the higher realm of my own thinking.'

Blofeld was a big man, perhaps six foot three, and power-fully built. He placed the tip of the *samurai* sword, which has almost the blade of the scimitar, between his straddled feet, and rested his sinewy hands on its boss. Looking up at him from across the room, Bond had to admit that there was some-thing larger than life in the looming, imperious figure, in the hypnotically direct stare of the eyes, in the tall white brow, in the cruel downward twist of the thin lips. The square-cut, heavily draped kimono, designed to give the illusion of bulk to a race of smallish men, made something huge out of the towering figure, and the golden dragon embroidery, so easily to be derided as a childish fantasy, crawled menacingly across the black silk and seemed to spit real fire from over the left breast. Blofeld had paused in his harangue. Waiting for him to continue, Bond took the measure of his enemy. He knew what would be coming – justification. It was always so. When they thought they had got you where they wanted you, when they knew they were decisively on top, before the knock-out, even to an audience on the threshold of extinction, it was pleasant, reassuring to the executioner, to deliver his apologia – purge the sin he was about to commit. Blofeld, his hands relaxed on the boss of his sword, continued. The tone of his voice was reasonable, self-assured, quietly expository.

He said, 'Now, Mister Bond, take Operation Thunderball, as your Government dubbed it. This project involved the holding to ransom of the Western World by the acquisition by me of two atomic weapons. Where lies the crime in this, except in the Erewhon of international politics? Rich boys are playing with rich toys. A poor boy comes along and takes them and offers them back for money. If the poor boy had been successful, what a valuable by-product might have resulted for the whole world. These were dangerous toys which, in the poor boy's hands, or let us say, to discard the allegory, in the hands of a Castro, could lead to the wanton extinction of mankind. By my action, I gave a dramatic example for all to see. If I had been successful and the money had been handed over, might not the threat of a recurrence of my attempt have led to serious disarmament talks, to an abandonment of these dangerous toys that might so easily get into the wrong hands? You follow my reasoning? Then this recent matter of the bacteriological warfare attack on England. My dear Mister Bond, England is a sick nation by any standards. By hastening the sickness to the brink of death, might Britain not have been forced out of her lethargy into the kind of community effort we witnessed during the war? Cruel to be kind, Mister Bond. Where lies the great crime there? And now this matter of my so-called "Castle of Death".' Blofeld paused and his eyes took on an inward look. He said, 'I will make a confession to you, Mister Bond. I have come to suffer from a certain lassitude of mind which I am determined to combat. This comes in part from being a unique genius who is alone in the world, without honour – worse, misunderstood. No doubt much of the root cause of this accidie is physical – liver, kidneys, heart, the usual weak points of the middle-aged. But there has developed in me a certain mental lameness, a disinterest in humanity and its future, an utter boredom with the affairs of mankind. So, not unlike the gourmet, with his jaded palate, I now seek only the highly spiced, the sharp impact on the taste buds, mental as well as physical, the tickle that is truly exquisite. And so, Mister Bond, I came to devise this useful and essentially humane project – the offer of free death to those who seek release from the burden of being alive. By doing so, I have not only provided the common man with a solution to the problem of whether to be or not to be, I have also provided the Japanese Government, though for the present they appear to be blind to my magnanimity, with a tidy, out-of-the-way charnel-house which relieves them of a constant flow of messy occurrences involving the trains, the trams, the volcanoes and other unattractively public means of killing yourself. You must admit that, far from being a crime, this is a public service unique in the history of the world.'

'I saw one man being disgustingly murdered yesterday.'

'Tidying up, Mister Bond. Tidying up. The man came here

wishing to die. What you saw done was only helping a weak
man to his seat on the boat across the Styx. But I can see that
we have no contact. I cannot reach what serves you for a
mind. For your part, you cannot see further than the simple
gratification of your last cigarette. So enough of this idle
chatter. You have already kept us from our beds far too long.
Do you want to be hacked about in a vulgar brawl, or will
you offer your neck in the honourable fashion?' Blofeld took
a step forward and raised his mighty sword in both hands and
held it above his head. The light from the oil lamps shimmered
on the blade and showed up the golden filigree engraving.

Bond knew what to do. He had known as soon as he had
been led back into the room and had seen the wounded
guard's stave still standing in the shadowed angle of the wall.
But there was a bell-push near the woman. She would have
to be dealt with first! Had he learned enough of the thrusts
and parries of *bojutsu* from the demonstration at the *ninja*
training camp? Bond hurled himself to the left, seized the
stave and leaped at the woman whose hand was already
reaching upwards.

The stave thudded into the side of her head and she
sprawled grotesquely forward off her chair and lay still.
Blofeld's sword whistled down, inches from his shoulder.
Bond twisted and lunged to his full extent, thrusting his stave
forward in the groove of his left hand almost as if it had been
a billiard cue. The tip caught Blofeld hard on the breast-
bone and flung him against the wall, but he hurtled back and
came inexorably forward, swishing his sword like a scythe.
Bond aimed at his right arm, missed and had to retreat. He
was concentrating on keeping his weapon as well as his body
away from the whirling steel, or his stave would be cut like
a matchstick, and its extra length was his only hope of victory.
Blofeld suddenly lunged, expertly, his right knee bent forward. Bond feinted to the left, but he was inches too slow
and the tip of the sword flicked his left ribs, drawing blood.
But before Blofeld could withdraw, Bond had slashed two-
handed, sideways, at his legs. His stave met bone. Blofeld
cursed, and made an ineffectual stab at Bond's weapon. Then

he advanced again and Bond could only dodge and feint in the middle of the room and make quick short lunges to keep the enemy at bay. But he was losing ground in front of the whirling steel, and now Blofeld, scenting victory, took lightning steps and thrust forward like a snake. Bond leaped sideways, saw his chance and gave a mighty sweep of his stave. It caught Blofeld on his right shoulder and drew a curse from him. His main sword arm! Bond pressed forward, lancing again and again with his weapon and scoring several hits to the body, but one of Blofeld's parries caught the stave and cut off that one vital foot of extra length as if it had been a candle-end. Blofeld saw his advantage and began attacking, making furious forward jabs that Bond could only parry by hitting at the flat of the sword to deflect it. But now the stave was slippery in the sweat of his hands and for the first time he felt the cold breath of defeat at his neck. And Blofeld seemed to smell it, for he suddenly executed one of his fast running lunges to get under Bond's guard. Bond guessed the distance of the wall behind him and leaped backwards against it. Even so he felt the sword-point fan across his stomach. But, hurled back by his impact with the wall, he counter-lunged, swept the sword aside with his stave and, dropping his weapon, made a dive for Blofeld's neck and got both hands to it. For a moment the two sweating faces were almost up against each other. The boss of Blofeld's sword battered into Bond's side. Bond hardly felt the crashing blows. He pressed with his thumbs, and pressed and pressed and heard the sword clank to the floor and felt Blofeld's fingers and nails tearing at his face, trying to reach his eyes. Bond whispered through his gritted teeth, 'Die, Blofeld! Die!' And suddenly the tongue was out and the eyes rolled upwards and the body slipped down to the ground. But Bond followed it and knelt, his hands cramped round the powerful neck, seeing nothing, hearing nothing, in the terrible grip of blood lust.

Bond slowly came to himself. The golden dragon's head on the black silk kimono spat flame at him. He unclasped his aching hands from round the neck and, not looking again at the purple face, got to his feet. He staggered. God, how his head hurt! What remained to be done? He tried to cast his mind back. He had had a clever idea. What was it? Oh yes, of course! He picked up Blofeld's sword and sleep-walked down the stone passage to the torture room. He glanced up at the clock. Five minutes to midnight. And there was the wooden box, mud-spattered, down beside the throne on which he had sat, days, years before. He went to it and hacked it open with one stroke of the sword. Yes, there was the big wheel he had expected! He knelt down and twisted and twisted until it was finally closed. What would happen now? The end of the world? Bond ran back up the passage. Now he must get out, get away from this place! But his line of retreat was closed by the guards! He tore aside a curtain and smashed the window open with his sword. Outside there was a balustraded terrace that seemed to run round this storey of the castle. Bond looked around for something to cover his nakedness. There was only Blofeld's sumptuous kimono. Coldly, Bond tore it off the corpse, put it on and tied the sash. The interior of the kimono was cold, like a snake's skin. He looked down at Irma Bunt. She was breathing heavily with a drunken snore. Bond went to the window and climbed out, minding his bare feet among the glass splinters.

But he had been wrong! The balustrade was a brief one, closed at both ends. He stumbled from end to end of it, but there was no exit. He looked over the side. A sheer hundred-foot drop to the gravel. A soft fluted whistle above him caught his ear. He looked up. Only a breath of wind in the moorings of that bloody balloon! But then a lunatic idea came to him, a flashback to one of the old Douglas Fairbanks films when the hero had swung across a wide hall by taking a flying leap at the chandelier. The helium balloon was strong enough to hold taut fifty feet of framed cotton strip bearing the warning sign! Why shouldn't it be powerful enough to bear the weight of a man?

Bond ran to the corner of the balustrade to which the mooring line was attached. He tested it. It was taut as a wire! From somewhere behind him there came a great clamour in the castle. Had the woman woken up? Holding on to the straining rope, he climbed on to the railing, cut a foothold for himself in the cotton banner and, grasping the mooring rope with his right hand, chopped downwards below him with Blofeld's sword and threw himself into space.

It worked! There was a light night breeze and he felt himself wafted gently over the moonlit park, over the glittering, steaming lake, towards the sea. But he was rising, not falling! The helium sphere was not in the least worried by his weight! Then blue-and-yellow fire fluttered from the upper storey of the castle and an occasional angry wasp zipped past him. Bond's hands and feet were beginning to ache with the strain of holding on. Something hit him on the side of the head, the same side that was already sending out its throbbing message of pain. And that finished him. He knew it had! For now the whole black silhouette of the castle swayed in the moonlight and seemed to jig upwards and sideways and then slowly dissolve like an icecream cone in sunshine. The top storey crumbled first, then the next, and the next, and then, after a moment, a huge jet of orange fire shot up from hell towards the moon and a buffet of hot wind, followed by an echoing crack of thunder, hit Bond and made his balloon sway violently.

What was it all about? Bond didn't know or care. The pain in his head was his whole universe. Punctured by a bullet, the balloon was fast losing height. Below, the softly swelling sea offered a bed. Bond let go with hands and feet and plummeted down towards peace, towards the rippling feathers of some childhood dream of softness and escape from pain.

21

OBIT:

THE ✤✤✤✤✤ TIMES

COMMANDER JAMES BOND,
CMG, RNVR

M. WRITES:

As your readers will have learned from earlier issues, a senior officer of the Ministry of Defence, Commander James Bond, CMG, RNVR, is missing, believed killed, while on an official mission to Japan. It grieves me to have to report that hopes of his survival must now be abandoned. It therefore falls to my lot, as the Head of the Department he served so well, to give some account of this officer and of his outstanding services to his country.

James Bond was born of a Scottish father, Andrew Bond of Glencoe, and a Swiss mother, Monique Delacroix, from the Canton de Vaud. His father being a foreign representative of the Vickers armaments firm, his early education, from which he inherited a first-class command of French and German, was entirely abroad. When he was eleven years of age, both his parents were killed in a climbing accident in the Aiguilles Rouges above Chamonix, and the youth came under the guardianship of an aunt, since deceased, Miss Charmian Bond, and went to live with her at the quaintly-named hamlet of Pett Bottom near Canterbury in Kent. There, in a small cottage hard by the attractive Duck Inn, his aunt, who must have been a most erudite and accomplished lady, completed his education for an English public school, and, at the age of twelve or thereabouts, he passed satisfactorily into Eton, for which College he had been entered at birth by his father. It must be admitted that his career at Eton was brief and undistinguished and, after only two halves, as a result, it pains me to record, of some alleged trouble with one of the boys' maids, his aunt was requested to remove him. She managed to obtain his transfer to Fettes, his father's old school. Here the atmosphere was somewhat Calvinistic, and both academic and athletic standards were rigorous. Nevertheless, though inclined to be solitary by nature, he established some firm friendships among the traditionally famous athletic circles at the school. By the time he left, at the early age of seventeen, he had twice fought for the school as a light-weight and had, in addition, founded the first serious judo class at a British public school. By now it was 1941 and, by claiming an age of nineteen and with the help of an old Vickers colleague of his father, he entered a branch of what was subsequently to become the Ministry of Defence. To serve the confidential nature of his duties, he was accorded the rank of lieutenant in the Special Branch of the RNVR, and it is a measure of the satisfaction his services gave to his superiors that he ended the war with the rank of Commander. It was about this time that the writer became associated with certain aspects of the Ministry's work, and it was with much gratification that I accepted Commander Bond's post-war application to continue working for the Ministry in which, at the time of his lamented disappearance, he had risen to the rank of Principal Officer in the Civil Service.

The nature of Commander Bond's duties with the Ministry, which were, incidentally, recognized by the appointment of CMG in 1954, must remain confidential, nay secret, but his colleagues at the Ministry will allow that he performed them with outstanding bravery and distinction, although occasionally, through an impetuous strain in his nature, with a streak of the foolhardy that brought him in conflict with higher authority. But he possessed what almost amounted to 'The Nelson Touch' in moments of the highest emergency, and he somehow contrived to escape more or less unscathed from the many adventurous paths down which his duties led him. The inevitable publicity, particularly in the foreign Press, accorded some of these adventures, made him, much against his will, something of a public figure, with the inevitable result that a series of popular books came to be written around him by a personal friend and former colleague of James Bond. If the quality of these books, or their degree of veracity, had been any higher, the author would certainly have been prosecuted under the Official Secrets Act. It is a measure of the disdain in which these fictions are held at the Ministry, that action has not yet – I emphasize the qualification – been taken against the author and publisher of these high-flown and romanticized caricatures of episodes in the career of an outstanding public servant.

It only remains to conclude this brief *in memoriam* by assuring his friends that Commander Bond's last mission was one of supreme importance to the State. Although it now appears that, alas, he will not return from it, I have the authority of the highest quarters in the land to confirm that the mission proved one hundred per cent successful. It is no exaggeration to pronounce unequivocally that, through the recent valorous efforts of this one man, the Safety of the Realm has received mighty reassurance.

James Bond was briefly married in 1962, to Teresa, only daughter of Marc-Ange Draco, of Marseilles. The marriage ended in tragic circumstances that were reported in the Press at the time. There was no issue of the marriage and James Bond leaves, so far as I am aware, no relative living.

M. G. writes:

I was happy and proud to serve Commander Bond in a close capacity during the past three years at the Ministry of Defence. If indeed our fears for him are justified, may I suggest these simple words for his epitaph? Many of the junior staff here feel they represent his philosophy: 'I shall not waste my days in trying to prolong them. I shall use my time.'

22

SPARROWS' TEARS

WHEN Kissy saw the figure, black-winged in its kimono, crash down into the sea, she sensed that it was her man, and she covered the two hundred yards from the base of the wall as fast as she had ever swum in her life. The tremendous impact with the water had at first knocked all the wind out of Bond, but the will to live, so nearly extinguished by the searing pain in his head, was revived by the new but recognizable enemy of the sea and, when Kissy got to him, he was struggling to free himself from the kimono.

At first he thought she was Blofeld and tried to strike out at her.

'It's Kissy,' she said urgently, 'Kissy Suzuki! Don't you remember?'

He didn't. He had no recollection of anything in the world but the face of his enemy and of the desperate urge to smash it. But his strength was going and finally, cursing feebly, he allowed her to manhandle him out of the kimono and paid heed to the voice that pleaded with him.

'Now follow me, Taro-san. When you get tired I will pull you with me. We are all trained in such rescue work.'

But, when she started off, Bond didn't follow her. Instead he swam feebly round and round like a wounded animal, in ever-increasing circles. She almost wept. What had happened to him? What had they done to him at the Castle of Death? Finally she stopped him and talked softly to him and he docilely allowed her to put her arms under his armpits and, with his head cradled between her breasts, she set off with the traditional backward leg-stroke.

It was an amazing swim for a girl – half a mile with currents to contend with and only the moon and an occasional glance over her shoulder to give her a bearing, but she achieved it and finally hauled Bond out of the water in her little cove and collapsed on the flat stones beside him.

She was awoken by a groan from Bond. He had been quietly sick and now sat with his head in his hands, looking blankly out to sea with the glazed eyes of a sleepwalker. When Kissy put an arm round his shoulders, he turned vaguely towards her. 'Who are you? How did I get here? What is this place?' He examined her more carefully. 'You're very pretty.'

Kissy looked at him keenly. She said, and a sudden plan of great glory blazed across her mind, 'You cannot remember anything? You do not remember who you are and where you came from?'

Bond passed a hand across his forehead, squeezed his eyes. 'Nothing,' he said wearily. 'Nothing except a man's face. I think he was dead. I think he was a bad man. What is your name? You must tell me everything.'

'My name is Kissy Suzuki and you are my lover. Your name is Taro Todoroki. We live on this island and go fishing together. It is a very good life. But can you walk a little? I must take you to where you live and get you some food and a doctor to see you. You have a terrible wound on the side of your head and there is a cut on your ribs. You must have fallen while you were climbing the cliffs after seagulls' eggs.' She stood up and held out her hands.

Bond took them and staggered to his feet. She held him by the hand and gently guided him along the path towards the Suzuki house. But she passed it and went on and up to the grove of dwarf maples and camellia bushes. She led him behind the Shinto shrine and into the cave. It was large and the earth floor was dry. She said, 'This is where you live. I live here with you. I had put away our bed things. I will go and fetch them and some food. Now lie down, my beloved, and rest and I will look after you. You are ill, but the doctor will make you well again.'

Bond did as he was told and was instantly asleep, the pain-free side of his head cradled on his arm.

Kissy ran off down the mountain, her heart singing. There

was much to be done, much to be arranged, but now she had got her man back she was desperately determined to keep him.

It was almost dawn and her parents were awake. She whispered to them excitedly as she went about warming some milk and putting together a bundle of *futon*, her father's best kimono and a selection of Bond's washing things – nothing to remind him of his past. Her parents were used to her whims and her independence. Her father merely commented mildly that it would be all right if the *kannushi-san* gave his blessing, then, having washed the salt off herself and dressed in her own simple brown kimono, she scampered off up the hill to the cave.

Later, the Shinto priest received her gravely. He almost seemed to be expecting her. He held up his hand and spoke to the kneeling figure. 'Kissy-chan, I know what I know. The spawn of the devil is dead. So is his wife. The Castle of Death has been totally destroyed. These things were brought about as the Six Guardians foretold, by the man from across the sea. Where is he now?'

'In the cave behind the shrine, *kannushi-san*. He is gravely wounded. I love him. I wish to keep him and care for him. He remembers nothing of the past. I wish it to remain so, so that we may marry and he may become a son of Kuro for all time.'

'That will not be possible, my daughter. In due course he will recover and go off across the world to where he came from. And there will be official inquiries for him, from Fukuoka, perhaps even from Tokyo, for he is surely a man of renown in his own country.'

'But *kannushi-san*, if you so instruct the elders of Kuro, they will show these people *shiran-kao*, they will say they know nothing, that this man Todoroki left, swimming for the mainland, and has not been heard of since. Then the people will go away. All I want to do is to care for him and keep him for myself as long as I can. If the day comes when he wishes to leave, I will not hinder him. I will help him. He was happy here fishing with me and my David-bird. He told me so. When he recovers, I will see that he continues to be happy.

Should not Kuro cherish and honour this hero who was brought to us by the gods? Would not the Six Guardians wish to keep him for a while? And have I not earned some small token for my humble efforts to help Todoroki-san and save his life?'

The priest sat silent for a while with his eyes closed. Then he looked down at the pleading face at his feet. He smiled. 'I will do what is possible, Kissy-chan. And now bring the doctor to me and then take him up to the cave so that he can tend this man's wounds. Then I will speak to the elders. But for many weeks you must be very discreet and the *gaijin* must not show himself. When all is quiet again, he may move back into the house of your parents and allow himself to be seen.'

The doctor knelt beside Bond in the cave and spread out on the ground a large map of the human head with the sections marked with figures and ideograms. His gentle fingers probed Bond's wounds for signs of fracture, while Kissy knelt beside him and held one of Bond's sweating hands in both of hers. The doctor bent forward and, lifting the eyelids one by one, gazed deeply into the glazed eyes through a large reading-glass. On his instructions, Kissy ran for boiling water, and the doctor proceeded to clean the cut made by the bullet across the terrible swelling of the first wound caused by Bond's crash into the oubliette. Then he tapped sulpha dust into the wound and bound up the head neatly and expertly, put surgical plaster over the cut across the ribs and stood up and took Kissy outside the cave. 'He will live,' he said, 'but it may be months, even years before he regains his memory. It is particularly the temporal lobe of his brain, where the memory is stored, that has been damaged. For this, much education will be necessary. You will endeavour all the time to remind him about past things and places. Then isolated facts that he will recognize will turn into chains of association. He should undoubtedly be taken to Fukuoka for an X-ray, but I think there is no fracture and in any case the *kannushi-san* has ordained that he is to remain under your care and his presence on the island to be kept secret. I shall of course observe the instructions of the honourable *kannushi-san* and only visit him by different routes and at night. But there is much you will have to attend to for he must not be moved in any way for at least a week. Now listen carefully,' said the doctor, and gave her minute instructions which covered every aspect of feeding and nursing and left her to carry them out.

And so the days ran into weeks and the police came again and again from Fukuoka, and the official called Tanaka came from Tokyo and later a huge man who said he was from Australia arrived and he was the most difficult of all for Kissy to shake off. But the face of *shiran-kao* remained of stone and the island of Kuro kept its secret. James Bond's body gradually mended and Kissy took him out for walks at night. They also went for an occasional swim in the cove, where they played with David and she told him all the history of the Ama and of Kuro and expertly parried all his questions about the world outside the island.

Winter came, and the Ama had to stay ashore and turn their hands to mending nets and boats and working on the smallholdings on the mountain side, and Bond came back into the house and made himself useful with carpentry and odd jobs and with learning Japanese from Kissy. The glazed look went from his eyes, but they remained remote and far-away and every night he was puzzled by dreams of a quite different world of white people and big cities and half-remembered faces. But Kissy assured him that these were just nightmares such as she had, and that they had no meaning, and gradually Bond came to accept the little stone-and-wood house and the endless horizon of sea as his finite world. Kissy was careful to keep him away from the south coast of the island, and dreaded the day when fishing would begin again at the end of May and he would see the great black wall across the straits and memory might come flooding back.

The doctor was surprised by Bond's lack of progress and resigned himself to the conclusion that Bond's amnesia was total, but soon there was no cause for further visits because Bond's physical health and his apparently complete satisfaction with his lot showed that in every other respect he was totally recovered.

But there was one thing that greatly distressed Kissy. From the first night in the cave she had shared Bond's *futon* and, when he was well and back in the house, she waited every night for him to make love to her. But, while he kissed her occasionally and often held her hand, his body seemed totally unaware of her however much she pressed herself against him and even caressed him with her hands. Had the wound made him impotent? She consulted the doctor, but he said there could be no connexion, although it was just possible that he had forgotten how to perform the act of love.

So one day Kissy Suzuki announced that she was going to take the weekly mailboat to Fukuoka to do some shopping and, in the big city, she found her way to the local sex-shop, called The Happy Shop, that is a feature of all self-respecting Japanese towns, and told her problem to the wicked-looking old greybeard behind the innocent counter containing nothing more viciously alluring than tonics and contraceptives. He asked her if she possessed five thousand yen, which is a lot of money, and when she said she did, he locked the street door and invited her to the back of the shop.

The sex merchant bent down and pulled out from beneath a bench what looked like a small wired rabbit-hutch. He put this on the bench and Kissy saw that it contained four large toads on a bed of moss. Next he produced a metal contraption that had the appearance of a hot-plate with a small wire cage in the middle. He carefully lifted out one of the toads and placed it inside the cage so that it squatted on the metal surface. Then he hauled a large car battery on to the bench, put it alongside the 'hot-plate' and attached wires from one to the other. Then he spoke some encouraging endearments to the toad and stood back.

The toad began to shiver slightly, and the crosses in its dark red eyes blazed angrily at Kissy as if it knew it was all her fault. The sex merchant, his head bent over the little cage, watched anxiously and then rubbed his hands with satisfaction as heavy beads of sweat broke out all over the toad's warty skin. He reached for an iron teaspoon and a small phial, gently raised the wire cage and very carefully scraped the sweat-beads off the toad's body and dripped the result into the phial. When he had finished, the phial contained about half a teaspoon of clear liquid. He corked it up and handed it to Kissy, who held it with reverence and great care as if it had been a fabulous jewel. Then the sex merchant disconnected the wires and put the toad, which seemed none the worse for its experience, back in its hutch and closed the top.

He turned to Kissy and bowed. 'When this valuable product is desired by a sincere customer I always ask them to witness the process of distillation. Otherwise they might harbour the unworthy thought that the phial contained only water from the tap. But you have now seen that this preparation is the authentic sweat of a toad. It is produced by giving a toad a mild electric shock. The toad suffered only temporary dis-comfort and it will be rewarded this evening with an extra portion of flies or crickets. And now,' he went to a cupboard and took out a small pill-box, 'here is powder of dried lizard. A combination of the two, inserted in your lover's food at the evening meal, should prove infallible. However, to excite his mind as well as his senses, for an extra thousand yen I can provide you with a most excellent pillow-book.'

'What is a pillow-book?'

The sex merchant went back to his cupboard and pro-duced a cheaply bound and printed paper book with a plain cover. Kissy opened it. Her hand went to her mouth and she blushed furiously. But then, being a careful girl who didn't want to be cheated, she turned some more of the pages. They all contained outrageously pornographic close-up pictures, most faithfully engraved, of the love-act portrayed from every possible aspect. 'Very well,' she whispered. She handed back the book. 'Please wrap up everything carefully.' She took out her purse and began counting out the notes.

Out in the shop, the wicked-faced old man handed her the parcel and, bowing deeply, unlocked the door. Kissy gave a perfunctory bob in return and darted out of the shop down the street as if she had just made a pact with the devil.

But by the time she went to catch the mailboat back to Kuro, she was hugging herself with excitement and pleasure and making up a story to explain away her acquisition of the book.

Bond was waiting for her on the jetty. It was the first day she had been away from him and he had missed her painfully. They talked happily as they walked hand-in-hand along the foreshore among the nets and boats, and the people smiled to see them, but looked through them instead of greeting them for had not the priest decreed that their *gaijin* here did not officially exist? And the priest's edict was final.

Back at the house, Kissy went happily about preparing a highly spiced dish of *sukiyaki*, the national dish of beef stew. This was not only a great treat, for they seldom ate meat, but Kissy didn't know if her love-potions had any taste and it would be wise not to take any chances. When it was ready, with a trembling hand, she poured the brown powder and the liquid into Bond's portion and stirred it well. Then she brought the dishes in to where the family awaited, squatting on the *tatami* before the low table.

She watched surreptitiously as Bond devoured every scrap of his portion and wiped his plate clean with a pinch of rice and then, after warm compliments on her cooking, drank his tea and retired to their room. In the evenings, he usually sat mending nets or fishing lines before going to bed. As she helped her mother wash up she wondered if he were doing so now!

Kissy spent a long time doing her hair and making herself pretty before, her heart beating like a captured bird, she joined him.

He looked up from the pillow-book and laughed. 'Kissy, where in God's name did you get this?'

She giggled. 'Oh that! I forgot to tell you. Some dreadful man tried to make up to me in one of the shops. He pressed that into my hand and made an assignation for this evening. I agreed just to get rid of him. It is what we call a pillow-book. Lovers use them. Aren't the pictures exciting?'

Bond threw off his kimono. He pointed to the soft *futon* on the floor. He said fiercely, 'Kissy, take off your clothes and lie down there. We'll start at page one.'

Winter slid into spring and fishing began again, but now Kissy dived naked like the other girls and Bond and the bird dived with her and there were good days and bad days. But the sun shone steadily and the sea was blue and wild irises covered the mountain-side and everyone made a great fuss as the sprinkling of cherry trees burst into bloom, and Kissy wondered what moment to choose to tell Bond that she was going to have a baby and whether he would then propose marriage to her.

But one day, on the way down to the cove, Bond looked pre-occupied and, when he asked her to wait before they put the boat out as he had something serious to talk to her about, her heart leaped and she sat down beside him on a flat rock and put her arms round him and waited.

Bond took a crumpled piece of paper out of his pocket and held it out to her, and she shivered with fear and knew what was coming. She took her arms from round him and looked at the paper. It was one of the rough squares of newspaper from the spike in the little lavatory. She always tore these squares herself and discarded any that contained words in English – just in case.

Bond pointed. 'Kissy, what is this word "Vladivostok"? What does it mean? It has some kind of a message for me. I connect it with a very big country. I believe the country is called Russia. Am I right?'

Kissy remembered her promise to the priest. She put her face in her hands. 'Yes, Taro-san. That is so.'

Bond pressed his fists to his eyes and squeezed. 'I have a feeling that I have had much to do with this Russia, that a lot of my past life was concerned with it. Could that be possible? I long so terribly to know where I came from before I came to Kuro. Will you help me, Kissy?'

Kissy took her hands from her face and looked at him. She said quietly, 'Yes, I will help you, my beloved.'

'Then I must go to this place Vladivostok, and perhaps it

will awaken more memories and I can work my way back from there.'

'If you say so, my love. The mailboat goes to Fukuoka tomorrow. I will put you on a train there and give you money and full directions. It is advertised that one can go from the northern island, Hokkaido, to Sakhalin which is on the Russian mainland. Then you can no doubt make your way to Vladivostok. It is a great port to the south of Sakhalin. But you must take care, for the Russians are not friendly people.'

'Surely they would do no harm to a fisherman from Kuro?'

Kissy's heart choked her. She got up and walked slowly down to the boat. She pushed the boat down the pebbles into the water and waited, at her usual place in the stern, for him to get in and for his knees to clasp hers as they always did.

James Bond took his place and unshipped the oars, and the cormorant scrambled on board and perched imperiously in the bows. Bond measured where the rest of the fleet lay on the horizon and began to row.

Kissy smiled into his eyes and the sun shone on his back and, so far as James Bond was concerned, it was a beautiful day just like all the other days had been – without a cloud in the sky.

But then, of course, he didn't know that his name was James Bond. And, compared with the blazing significance to him of that single Russian word on the scrap of paper, his life on Kuro, his love for Kissy Suzuki, were, in Tiger's phrase, of as little account as sparrows' tears.

'A master of tantalising suspense'
THE BOOKMAN

Gavin Lyall

THE WRONG SIDE OF THE SKY   3/6

THE MOST DANGEROUS GAME   3/6

'Good thriller writers are born, not made.
They are one in a thousand — an Ambler,
a Fleming, a Hammond Innes — and Gavin
Lyall is unmistakably of their company.'
JOHN O'LONDON'S

Hammerhead   3/6

JAMES MAYO

The first of a series of thrillers featuring
CHARLES HOOD

Suave, accomplished, deadly — his
sophisticated mode of life camouflages his
career as the most coldly dangerous secret
agent in Europe.

'Excitement and violence is jet-propelled.
MANCHESTER EVENING NEWS